The not so Best Man

The not so Best Man

Copyright © 2024 Jessica Whaley
All Rights Reserved.

Cover Design by: Lyssa at Booked Forever Shop

Editing by: Pat Norton

Jessica Whaley
P.O. Box 785
Leesburg, Al. 35983
authorjdwhaley@gmail.com

ISBN 979-8-9906151-5-1 (Paperback)
ISBN 979-8-9906151-4-4 (Ebook)

<u>Also written by Jessica Whaley:</u>
(Available on Kindle Unlimited and Amazon)

- **The Maple Small Town Romance Series**

    - Letters To Magnolia (Book 1)
    - The Light in His Darkness (Book 2)

The not so Best Man

Notes from the Author:

If you are looking for an innocent Christmas Hallmark vibe book; this one is not it. This book holds flashbacks of a broken home, suicidal thoughts, parental abuse, and a love that gets broken.

Though it does have a happily ever after along with some scenes that may make you blush; this book does contain triggers. While it is a story that is centered around Christmas time… it is not about Christmas as a whole. I trust you know your triggers before reading.

I truly loved writing Macy and Jordans story. In the end, the story does finally come full circle for them. I hope you curl up with your favorite blanket, a cup of your favorite beverage, and enjoy it all.

This is a quick and easy read. I intended it to be that way. Short and sweet.

When you meet Kyla and Pinky, I hope you love them as much as I loved writing about them.

Trigger Warnings:
Talk of suicide
Parental Abuse: both physical and mental
Fighting and Punching
Close spaces in Escape Room
Creepy Elves

Dedication:

For my readers who love Christmas and spicy books. We are all on Santa's naughty list this year.

Chapter One
Macy

"Macy, I swear to god if you are late getting here, I am going to kill you."

"Oh, bite me, Paige." I tell my sister, "Once I'm done with my final, I will be jumping on the plane to Colorado for your precious Christmas wedding week." I say sarcastically into the phone. I cannot stand Christmas Day anymore but for her I'll endure the endless activities set for this week. She has always loved Christmas time and her dream has forever been to get married on Christmas Day.

Paige huffs, "I mean it. You are my maid of honor. You have duties. I need you here." She is starting to pout making me roll my eyes in annoyance.

"I promise, I will be there." I pause, "Don't try to set me up with any of the groomsmen either!" I state to her, but it sounds like paper is crinkling on the other end.

"What? I cannot hear you. Love you, bye!" And with that sentence, Paige ends the phone call. I sigh, typical Paige. She is always trying to hook me up with her fiancé's, Dylan, friends. They are all stuck in their frat boy stage and definitely not my type.

I have given her an excuse every time she would bring one of them up; honestly, I have not dated anyone since high school. I wanted a fresh start and that meant in the dating department too. Plus, all Dylans friends are womanizers and only after one thing.

I'm so not looking forward to being around any of these groomsmen, but for my sister, I will put up with it for the week at-least. I am in my last semester getting my bachelor's in business. After high school, I wanted no part of our small town anymore. I had my heart set on one guy my whole high school career, yet even he managed to use me and break my heart in the end. My senior year of high school was the worst year of my life. All because of *him.* So, when that acceptance letter from CULA in California came around, I jumped on it along with the full four-year scholarship. Of course, I miss my sister and parents, but I believe moving off for a little while was healing, especially because of the hell I was put through in high school. I got a lease on an apartment on campus and got to experience life by myself. I have made a few friends within my major but the last four years was about learning myself. My wants, my needs, my personality. I wanted to learn to be on my own and make my own decisions. I was in control of it all and had no one else to stir me the other way.

Once I take my last final tomorrow, I will be free of school forever and ready to receive my diploma at graduation next spring. It worked out perfectly because I can take my final and then board the plane to Colorado for my sister's Christmas Wedding where I will be her Maid of Honor. A friend of mine is taking over my apartment lease and most of my things are already moved back home. My dad says after the wedding we will come back for the things left in the storage container.

The best part about going to Colorado is the simple fact of, *he will not be there.*

Ring. Ring.

I look up from my computer where I am studying for my final and see my mothers name light up on my phone. Sliding it to answer I say, "Hey mom."

"Honey! How are finals?" She asks cheerfully.

"Take my last one tomorrow morning." I say vaguely.

"Great! Got your ticket?" She asks.

I roll my eyes, "Yes mom, I will meet you all there tomorrow. Flight should only take an hour."

My parents rented a chalet in the mountains of Colorado about twenty minutes closer to the wedding venue since Paige wanted the whole bridal party staying together for the week leading up to the wedding weekend. Apparently, she has even hired a wedding planner who has a full itinerary for us, not sure what my duties of Maid of Honor include if this woman has everything planned out already.

"Call me after class, when you board, and soon as you land. The chalet is gorgeous, honey! I think you will love it. There are plenty of handsome men coming." I can picture her smiling on the other end. This woman thinks I need to be in a relationship so bad she cannot stand it.

"Mom, I am not hooking up with no one at this wedding." I sternly tell her.

"You need to de stress, Macy." She laughs.

I want this conversation to be over with, NOW. "Goodbye mother. I will call you tomorrow. Love you."

"Oh honey. You are an adult. It is perfectly normal. I love you too." She laughs and hangs up the phone.

Placing my phone on the counter, I hold my hand to steady my forehead as I lean on the kitchen bar where I'm studying – *A whole week with this woman is going to drive me insane.*

Ding. An email comes through my computer, making me jump. I quickly open it.

Miss Cambron,

I am pleased to inform you of your excellent grade point average for this semester. You are exempt from the final tomorrow. I have already sent off your grades for the graduation committee and hope to see wonderful things from you in the business world. If you need anything along the way, please do not hesitate to reach out. Enjoy your Christmas and New Year!

Sincerely,
Professor Allen

I jump to my feet and re read the email repeatedly.

I cannot believe this! Jumping up and down I grab my phone and call Paige.

"Hello?" She answers.

"Get ready, bitch! I'm heading your way!"

It sounds like she knocked something over on her end and squeals, "No freaking way!"

"I'm exempt from my final. I just got the email! I'm packing my bags now and going to trade my ticket in for an earlier flight!"

"Get your ass down here! I cannot wait to hug your neck!" She yells in the phone, and I can hear my mother in the background asking what is going on, "Macy is getting to come down early!!" She screams at mom, busting my ear drum. I jerk the phone from my ear laughing.

"Tell her why so she doesn't freak out." I make sure to tell her.

She laughs and I can hear my mom jumping up and down in the background. It has been a few months since I have been home. Classes and internships have kept me busy; it has not been possible. Honestly, I have not made much of an effort to go home either. Too many memories, and people I would much rather stay away from.

"Don't forget your dress!" Paige yells into the phone, "Be safe and call us as soon as you land!" She orders me.

We hang up the phone and I run into my room and start packing my bag, making sure to grab my emerald green maid of honor dress that is hanging in the closet, all my utilities, and shoes. Within an hour I am ready to go and call an Uber to meet me out front. I have paid for my car to be in storage with the rest of my belongings until I get back, so no need to drive to the air port.

Colorado here I come.

Shit. I do not own a winter jacket anymore...

Chapter Two
Jordan

"Yeah man, I am going to be there!" I tell Dylan, my best friend, on the phone as I am packing my bag for the week.

At first, I did not think I was going to be able to make it to his wedding this weekend. I am a lead Engineer for a worldwide plant that makes airplane parts. Getting time off is not necessarily a benefit I have even when I know dates in advance, but a certain text message I got a month ago has me on edge. I contemplated on quitting my job if that was what I had to do to make sure I was at this wedding. I had not received any updates from this particular phone number in awhile but reading his words through text made my adrenaline skyrocket.

Thankfully, As luck would have it, I was able to get a last minute fill in for my position with a colleague I went to school with; we will ignore the fact that I basically bribed him with an extra couple thousand dollars of pay under the table if he would do it without asking questions.

I am anxious to see *her*. I know she will be there; she is the bride's maid of honor AND her sister. I have not seen Macy in years, but I keep up with her through our instagrams and mutual friends. Silently, I watch her post and without interacting with any of her photos, I do look at them. She has grown up a lot over the past few years. She hates me, for things I truly deserve to be hated for. If she only knew the truth of why I had to do what I did, I hope she would understand. Some things though, you can never ask someone to forgive you for, no matter how much you want to; just because of how bad it was. That is how it feels between us anyway.

The worst part, no one knows my secret besides Dylan and I.

"I am so relieved." Dylan says on the other end of the phone, "Greg being my best man was not what I had in mind. So glad you will be there. How were you able to get it covered? I know what you do for a job is not easy to get time off."

"Let's just say, I'm losing money on the deal." I say nonchalantly.

Dylan laughs, "Whatever it takes, man."

I smile, thankful for Dylan and our lifelong friendship. He has been like a brother to me since he jumped on my fathers back when he walked by our house one Saturday on a morning run watching him beat the shit out of me in our front yard. After that day, I spent more time at his house than my own. Though I never truly knew when my next beating would be, I knew I had an escape. They were the second family I never knew I needed, especially after my mother died and my life will always be the way it is because of them.

Well, my second family and *Macy.*

I have a lot of regrets when it comes to that girl- that woman.

"Is the whole wedding party going to be there?" I ask nonchalantly trying to not make it obvious that I am asking about her.

Dylan sighs, "Yeah I think so." He pauses and then he sighs again, more intense this time, "About that man, we need to have a talk before you get here."

I rub my hand over my face knowing where this is going, "I need you to be on your best behavior. Paige would kill me if this week and weekend gets ruined over nonsense. If you try to get Macy or Paige in a bad mood while you are here, I will personally ask you to leave. If you care anything about me, please refrain from acting out to get Macy's attention."

I'm shocked at his last sentence, "I don't know what you are talking about."

He huffs, "Jordan, I am serious. I know she was once the girl of your dreams. I know you have missed seeing her. She has grown up into quite the young woman now. So, when you see her and must be around her this week, I need you to remember you are there for one reason and that is for mine and Paige's wedding day, not to hit it and quit it with my sister-in-law. I will beat your ass If you try anything with her. You had your time with her, you do not get a second chance. I need you two to get along for the wedding's sake, that is it."

I roll my eyes, "Already acting like a protective big brother." I smirk.

"I mean it, Smith." His tone is clipped which means I need to quit joking.

"Believe me man, you have nothing to worry about." I promise.

"I doubt that." His voice's tone more jokingly now. "Now get your ass here." Dylan laughs into the phone.

We say our goodbyes and I place my phone on my nightstand while I finish packing my bags for the car ride. It is only a thirty-minute ride from my house to the chalet Macy's parents rented for all of us. After college, I decided to buy a house in our hometown where Macy, Dylan, and Paige and I grew up. Although some memories are painful to relive, they are also the same memories that saved my life, and I won't ever let them go.

Chapter Three
Macy

When we were children, Paige and I would play dress up acting out our wedding days – she always dreamed of a Christmas Wedding. The only thing I would protest to her was how fucking cold it would be on that day. As children, we both hated the snow, living in it will make you that way. We both said we wanted to live somewhere when we got older where it was sunny all the time. Colorado is miserably cold in December. The snow is only pretty in pictures. I grew up here my entire life somehow missing the gene for loving the powder of white that would fall from the sky and stay for weeks at a time or longer. When I moved off to California, I eventually gave away all my winter clothes because I did not plan to come back home much if ever.

Rolling luggage through the mounds of snow is not ideal, and I think my toes might fall off because my shoes are not snow proof and my feet are soaked.

I look a hot mess getting out of my Uber, that picked me up at the airport, after it pulls up at the chalet. I do not own a jacket because in California owning one is irrelevant. My shoes are for cute outfits not for hiking in feet of snow, and my brunette hair I'm sure has icicles hanging in it.

"You're not from here, are you?" The Uber driver asks, and I roll my eyes, "use to be. I just have not been home in a while."

He chuckles, "if you say so, miss." He points at my shoes buried under snow, "might want to grab some better shoes before your toes fall off."

I dismiss his statement grabbing my suitcase wheeling it to the front door while the Uber drives off. I look up in amazement; This place is huge. There is at-least ten bedrooms in this chalet and woods all around it keeping it secluded. Walking under the dark stone breezeway and out of the snow finally, I turn the knob on the front door, but it is locked. Thankfully, there is a doorbell. On the first ring, no one answers. Hitting the button a second try, the door finally opens.

"Macy!" Dylan, my sister's fiancé, says as the door swings opens.

"Hey D! Not to be rude, but I am freezing." I laugh and push past him. Once my luggage is in the door, I throw my arms around Dylan and give him a hug.

"Paige has been anxiously waiting on you." He tells me nervously and I look at him funny.

"What is going on?" I ask concerned and about that time Paige comes around the corner. Dylan nervously runs his hands through his hair.

"Hey sis!" Paige says throwing me into a hug.

"Cut the shit. What is going on?" I ask and they look at each other nervously.

"Well," my sister starts, but before she can finish her sentence, I see the issue staring right at me from the stairs.

Jordan. Fucking. Smith.

He is in a v neck blue T-shirt and blue jeans. His brown hair is a mess on top of his head, and he is holding a beer in his hand. Grinning at me like he's Gods gift to women or something.

What a jackass.

My sister pats me on the back and I look at her angrily, "What the hell is he doing here?" I ask sternly.

"Decided I could make the wedding after all, roomie." He smirks walking towards me, "nice outfit and hair." He says looking me up and down and walking past us into the other room.

I turn quickly to Dylan and Paige, "Why did he just call me roomie and what the fuck is he doing here? You told me months ago he said he was not going to be able to get off for this week."

Dylan runs his hand through his hair again and looks at Paige nervously.

She gives him a look of anger telling him, "Gee thanks for the backup." She turns to me and waves it off, "Okay look. I know it's not ideal, but Jordan was able to come and since he's Dylans best friend, he has been moved to Best Man again." She eyes me looking for my reaction.

"His best man? You mean I have to walk down the aisle with that fucker?" I yell at her pointing in the direction Jordan walked off in.

"Macy please, for me. Your sister. It's just one week. Then you're done with him forever. Besides, I know we were all close at one time. Just allow yourself to forgive him this week. Once the wedding is over, you can go back to hating him. I just need y'all to get along, please." She tells me pulling ice out of my hair. "I know Christmas is a sore spot for you both, but it is my wedding day and I am your big sister who loves you with all my heart."

This brat better be thankful I love her.

Her eyes and body language makes me sense she is keeping something else from me, "What else are you not telling me?" I ask them both and Dylan leaves us quickly walking in the direction Jordan went.

I scan my sister's eyes, and she takes a deep breath, "Okay. But remember you are my sister, and you love me. You can handle this."

"If you do not fucking spit it out right now so help me you won't have a maid of honor. I'll go my ass back to California." I tell her.

"Well, see, mom and dad rented this chalet back when they thought he was not coming. So it only occupied the family and bridle party that RSVP." She pauses and I do not like where this is going, "They put you and Jordan in a room together."

If literal smoke could come out of my ears, it would be roaring right now.

"Paige, you better be lying." I wag my finger at her.

"I'm sorry. Please, please for me. Just deal with it this week. He has promised me he would be on his best behavior and dad has already threatened him." She smiles at me, "of course you know mom has spoken her peace about him being hands on if he wants to be."

I swat at her and she giggles, "But seriously, Mace, for me, can you deal with him for the week? You will probably be in my room half the time anyways. The only reason I did not offer to share a room with you is because I knew Dylan would sneak in and I did not want to throw you out."

"Selfish brat." I grin, "You better know I love you."

She smiles and bear hugs me, "I love you more." Pulling back from me she scans my hair and outfit, "But first you need a shower and a new outfit."

"Yeah, about that. I think I under packed for this week. All of my winter clothes got thrown in the goodwill bag last year." I smirk.

Pulling my arm, she takes me up the stairs to my room and shows me where everything is. Jordan has already staked claim on things in our room, and it makes my blood boil seeing his things in here.

The room takes my breath away as we walk inside. There is a California king bed right in the center of the back wall, a big walk-in closet, the dresser has a tv in the back of it that you can turn down and hide inside the dresser or make pop out. But the bathroom is what makes me the giddiest. A full double waterfall walk in shower with marble tile, two vanity sinks, and a soaker jacuzzi tub. The white tile lines the floor, and the wall is a cream ivory. It would be perfect for a beach house to show off your tanned skin; so bright and luxurious.

"Towels are in the closet," Paige points in the direction and I nod, "come downstairs when you are done. I'll lay some clothes on the bed for you to change into until we can find you some warmer clothes for this week." she grins at me and walks out leaving me to myself.

When I turn to look in the mirror, I jump at the site of myself. I look like a rat and my hair is matted with ice hanging in it. Thankfully, I did not wear makeup on the plane. Pulling out all my hair and body care out of my bag I take my clothes off and put them in the hamper I found in the closet and turn the shower on stepping inside.

I do not care if I must share this room with Jordan. I will not let it ruin my sister's big day.

Chapter Four
Macy

"Honey! Im so glad you got here safely." My fathers voice comes into view entering the kitchen from my shower. I've washed and blown dry my hair, leaving loose curls behind my back. My makeup is light, mostly focusing on my blue eyes, and Paige laid me out some jeans and a white long sleeve shirt that melts to my skin and shows more cleavage than I would like. I'm fairly certain my sister is on a mission to get me laid too this week.

"Hey dad." I say walking up and hugging his neck. I'm such a daddy's girl and between both of my parents, my father is the one who has let me spread my wings the most. He understands me more than my mother. People have always said Paige took after my mother and I took after my father.

"Brian, move over and let me hug our girl." My moms soft voice comes through as she passes my father and hugs me tight. My father smiles watching us hug.

"Hey mom." I say, "thanks for the heads up about a jacket." I joke.

She laughs, "You are the one who wanted to be treated like an adult. I figured you would have thought about it." She winks and I roll my eyes.

"Where is the rest of the bridal party?" I ask them and they both look at each other and back at me with concern, "Honey, I am so sorry about the rooming situation with Jordan." My mother says apologetically.

"I would have made his ass sleep outside if I had known." My father said sternly.

I know Jordan is like a second child to them. Dylan, Paige, Jordan, and I all basically grew up together. We went to high school together, birthday parties together, teenage years together. We were all four their children, until Jordan did what he did to me. My father still holds a little bit of a grudge. My mother on the other hand, secretly hoped we would always find our way back together.

I roll my eyes, "It's okay. I can deal with him for this week only."

"Oh Mace, maybe he can de stress you while you're sharing the bed." My mom winks at me and my face gets red with anger.

"Oh hush, Kristina." My fathers stern voice rises, "this is my daughter you are talking about."

"She is an adult Brian. It is perfectly normal, and she has been so stressed." She smiles at me, "just think about it."

I shake my head no, "Absolutely will not. I'm going to drink now." I say, excusing myself.

"Drinks are out on the patio dear." My mother informs me while turning back speaking to my father.

I exit out of the kitchen's double screen doors and out onto the covered patio. It's vacant of people but there is a mini bar that I'm sure my mother was referring to. Bending down to grab a wine cooler from the mini fridge behind the bar I'm startled when I hear a male voice.

"Someone's been working out."

Jordan.

I jump and stand straight up, straighten my shirt and pulling it up to try to cover my cleavage but it doesn't work because his eyes immediately leave mine and look right at my breast.

"Typical Jordan." I roll my eyes and look around for an opener.

"What Mace? Im just admiring your beauty. Speaking of, wet snow hair, not your best look." He smirks taking a sip of his beer.

"First off, it's Macy to you. And second, you have no right to speak about my body." Anger boils at me.

"Oh come on, when are you going to forgive me?" He pouts playfully.

I find what I'm looking for and quickly take off the top to my wine cooler. I sit it down on the bar and lean close to him, "Let's get one thing clear. I hate you. Will always hate you. You left me heart broken on one of my favorite days. Dragging me along all that time as I was just your play thing and the things I did for you; I stood up for you, Smith. I will never forgive you for the trauma you put my heart through but for my sister's sake, I will tolerate you this week. You as so much try anything stupid and I'll head back to California so fast. I was so looking forward to you not being here."

He just stares at me, lust in his eyes but I take my wine cooler and walk off from the patio and back inside the house.

I will not let him get to me. I can't. He has already broken my heart enough.

***

Five years ago

"Hey Mace," My sister calls to me in the cafeteria of our high school. She is carrying a tray full of today's lunch — tacos, cheese dip and chips, and a soda. "I'm going to sit with you today. Dylan and one of his new friends are getting their plates and coming over too."

I nod taking a big bite of my taco while she sits down across from me. Paige and Dylan are a grade above me but the way our lunch times are scheduled, I have about ten minutes with them before I have to go back to class. My sister, her boyfriend, and I are all real close so we always try to sit together when we can.

Dylan walks up beside Paige and sits his plate down beside her, "You can sit beside Mace." He instructs his new friend that I have neglected to look at yet while I'm enjoying my tacos.

"Are you sure it's safe? She sure is inhaling that food. She may bite me." The guy to my right says and I jerk my head fast to ask him who he is talking to.

When my eyes find his, we both are shocked. "Um, Hey." He tells me.

I swallow my food slowly and embarrassment rushes over me, finally I say, "Hey."

Dylan points back and forth between us, "Y'all know each other?"

"That's her. The girl who I met on the ridge." He tells him.

I give him a death glare, none of my family knew I was up there that night.

Paige goes to say something to me and I look at her, "Don't you dare or I'll tell dad about y'all's hiding spot."

She glares at me but decides to keep her mouth shut.

"So Jordan," my sister starts, "want to come over to our house this evening and hang out? Since you already know my sister, it will keep her from being the third wheel like she always is." Dylan and Paige laugh.

I roll my eyes.

Jordan looks at me but I ignore him, "Sure." He answers her.

I did not see Jordan after the night of the ridge. We went our separate ways and I knew I would not see him at school. So for him to just show up and randomly be friends with my sisters boyfriend? How is this my life. Did he tell Dylan what happened on the ridge? Or is that staying between us? I have so many questions and my brain is in shock.

Later that evening, the dismissal bell rings through the high school halls and we all flood out of our classrooms. I hurry to my locker, grab my books, put them in my backpack, and make my way to the exit doors to Paiges car.

Someone grabs my wrist and I'm suddenly being pulled in the opposite direction. All I see is the back of his head, but his touch is lighting a torch through my body instantly. His long, dark, messy hair, holy t-shirt, and beige shorts are making my heart thump a little louder than it should.

No one seems to notice us as we make our way to the end of the hall, everyone is too busy worried about getting home. He leads me into a doorway and I knew exactly where I am — the janitors closet.

The door shuts behind me, it's a tiny closet and I'm immediately pushed up near his chest.

He flips the lights on and says, "Did you tell anyone?"

I look at him confused, "Tell who? What?"

His eyes lock on mine and for a minute, they slide down to my lips, my heart rate speeds up. His eyes quickly go back to mine and he whispers, "Did you tell anyone what happened on the ridge?"

I shake my head, no. Then add, "That's not my story to tell."

He gives me a soft smile, "I went up there a few more times after we met. Looking for you."

My brain misfires, is he flirting with me?

"Well, I'm glad you are doing good now. Dylan is a good guy, I'm sure you both will be best friends before the school year ends." I tell him turning to walk out of the janitors closet.

"It's nice knowing I'll be seeing you around a lot more, Mace." He tells me when I open the door to walk out. Thankful no one was standing there watching us leave.

The not so Best Man

The way he said my nickname made every fiber of hair on my skin stand to attention. Parts of me wanted to stay in that tiny closet with him, but my brain was sending red flags all over my body.

***

Present Day

I make my way to the dining room as supper is being brought to the table. My parents have catered the whole week out for our dinner and tonight is an Italian night. I enter the dining room in my long satin maroon dress. The V cut in the front is elegant but shows enough cleavage that I would not feel comfortable bending too far over and my white heels give me just enough length to give my legs definition from the split in my dress that comes up to my thighs.

The dining room is full of people; the entire wedding party made their arrival throughout the day today. Kelly, who Paige met in nursing school, is a quirky young twenty something blonde who I would never let touch me with a needle or take care of me in the hospital. She is book smart, but common sense is long gone there. Rylee is a cowgirl from Georgia that my sister met randomly one day in college, and they became good friends. Elizabeth is the oldest out of all of us. She is a childhood friend of mine and Paige's. She is an elementary school teacher in our hometown. I take a deep breath as I get closer to them and put on my smile as a good maid of honor would do.

"I'm so glad to see you all!" I state standing close to the girls and hug Elizabeth.

"My Mace girl!" Elizabeth says hugging me back. Man, how I have missed her.

Kelly and Rylee both smile back at me. I turn to the men standing in the room and greet them.

Frank, Henry, and Greg all stand by the table with beer in their hands smiling at me seductively. I'm not looking forward to this. They are all friends Dylan met in college and Paige has tried her damnedest to set me up with each one of them.

"Hey Macey." Frank says walking up and reaches out to hug me. I give him my best fake smile and side hug him quickly.

"Man, you sure look beautiful." He says, eyeing me. Although I catch that he disrespectfully is not looking at my eyes. He is looking right at my cleavage.

I smile trying to be polite, "Thank you. I hope you all had safe travels today."

Greg, who thankfully takes his eyes away from my breast and looks me in the eye as he speaks, "Not too bad of a flight. This place is gorgeous."

I grin, "My parents are all about go big or go home."

Henry chuckles, "I bet you are the same way aren't you?" He says seductively. Obviously, he has had one too many beers.

"Evening gentleman." A male's voice comes up behind us and the men jump, their eyes moving to the man behind me.

"Jordan. Glad you could make it brother." Frank says looking nervous and Jordan smiles at me not acknowledging Frank as he puts his hand out to me, "May I escort you to your seat." He asks politely and I get the hint at what he is doing.

Giving him my best fake soft smile, I take his hand, "Good to see you boys." My eyes leave theirs and are back on Jordan. As soon as we are out of the groomsmen hearing I remove my hand from his quickly and look at him sternly, "Don't think this will get you on my good side."

He smirks, "Odd way to say thank you."

I roll my eyes, "Why did you save me from them anyhow?" I ask.

He is silent for a moment and pulls out my seat, "Those fuckers could not stop looking at your boobs, Macy. Not a single one had the respect to look you in the eye. I'm the only one who can look at your cleavage."

I laugh but he stays serious, "I mean it Mace."

"I don't know what games you are trying to play but quit it." I whisper to him taking a seat and smiling as my parents, Paige, and Dylan enter the room.

He sits down at the seat next to me and I huff. What the heck is his deal?

Chapter Five
Macy

"I'm so glad you all could come this week and celebrate these two." My mother says to us around the table lifting her champagne glass. Jordan is sitting next to me having a conversation with Dylan.

Paige smiles at me and leans into me, "I'm glad you two could put your differences aside for the week." She winks at me, and I roll my eyes.

"Anything for you dear sister." I bat my eyes sarcastically.

We all start to fix our plate, and different conversations break out across the table. I pick up some spaghetti noodles with tongs and reach for the sauce with meatballs. As my hand hits the dipping spoon, I feel a warm hand on me. Jordan and I reached for the sauce at the same time and our eyes lock. My cheeks turn pink, and I quickly move my hand back. The tingling in my arm is taking over from his touch.

"I-I'm sorry," I mumble, "Go ahead." I tell him gesturing to the sauce.

"Ladies first." He grins at me clearly loving this.

I roll my eyes, "Jordan, just go."

Neither of us move.

"Well since you two cannot decide. I'm just going to go instead." Paige says sarcastically and I bite my lower lip to keep from laughing.

Once she puts the spoon back in the bowl, I reach for it and pour the sauce over my noodles trying not to notice that Jordans eyes have not left my face this entire time.

"Are you going to stare at me all night?" I joke with him taking a bite out of my meatball.

"I'm just marveling at how such a tiny girl can take so much meat." He smirks at me.

My mouth flies open at his remark, and I swat my hand at his shoulder, "Better mind your manners, Smith. Oh wait, that's right. You do not care about anyone else but yourself." I say sternly. "I'm surprised you are even here since you love ruining Christmas for those who care about you."

He leans into me to whisper into my ear, I feel goosebumps on my arm, "Not everything you believe is true, Mace. Just remember, I care more than you would think."

And with that statement, I straighten up and go back to eating my meal as he fixes his plate.

This is going to be a long week.

***

"Sweetie, if he gives you any issues, you let me know." My father says sternly eyeing Jordan as he stands by the stairs talking to Dylan.

I nod my head, "I can take care of myself daddy. He will be sleeping on the floor."

"Good girl." My father says kissing my forehead and hugging me before we both go our separate ways to bed.

Everyone else has gone to their bedrooms tonight. Lucky for me, I have to walk to the same room as Jordan Smith. Dylan kisses my cheek as I come up to him by the stairs, "Night, Mace." He says then turns to Jordan, "It would be in your best interest to remember what I said." He sternly tells his best friend.

Jordan smirks at him but doesn't reply. Dylan walks off ahead of us on the stairs and I noticed he doesn't go to his room but to Paiges. I smile. Those two were meant to be together. Ever since high school they have been the couple everyone wanted to be. Dylan has always been like an older brother to me.

"What did he mean by that?" I ask Jordan reaching the top of the stairs walking down the hall to our room.

"He is just being a protective big brother is all." Jordan replies but doesn't sound too happy.

I reach our bedroom door first and open the door. Walking in, I can feel Jordan's eyes on me. The room suddenly feels smaller than it looks. For a huge room, it feels like a tiny cardboard box now that we are inside it together.

"You will sleep on the floor." I state sternly grabbing my night clothes in my hands and walking to the bathroom.

I hear Jordan chuckle as I reach the door and I turn around seeing he is undoing his tie and unbuttoning his shirt, "Why would I do such a thing when there is a perfectly nice bed right here." He says sitting down on it to untie his shoes.

"Because I can't trust you to keep your hands to yourself." I affirm.

He slowly takes off his shoes and then slowly shimmies his shirt down his shoulders and pulls his arms out of the sleeves.

I gulp.

He looks better than I remember. His abs are defined in all the right places and the perfect V is cut right above his pants. He looks like a man who works out multiple times a week and eats all the right things. As a boy in high school he was hot, but he was just that, a boy. His hair was shaggy, he was skinny, and his clothes were old. Now looking at the man in-front of me, he is a God. His hair is short, his muscles defined in all the right places, and he is taller now. I can feel my cheeks burning.

"As I recall, Macy, it's you that I worry about taking advantage of me." He grins at me, standing and unbuttoning his pants.

I turn quickly and run into the bathroom shutting the door. My heart rate is racing.

He is just trying to get to you.

I remind my self. *You know him, you know his cocky personality, you know his game, you know his ways. And you are a grown ass woman now who can play them better.*

I stand infront of the mirror. Admiring my makeup, my hair, and my breast.

He's not the guy in high school anymore and I am not the immature and naïve girl who let him shred my heart to shreds.

I am a woman, and it's about time he learns a lesson on who the boss is now. I have control over my life – not him. He cannot make the choices for me anymore.

I pull my dress off and throw it in the hamper by the shower. I had originally grabbed a pair of sleep shorts and tshirt for bed but now that I'm looking at myself in my thong, I'm ready to play into this game.

I sit the shorts on the counter and unclip my bra laying it on top of the shorts. Only leaving my thong on and putting my baggy tshirt on. I let it stop at my hips, my thong is visible and look in the mirror at my nipples while they pebble back at me in the mirror.

I smirk.

Let the games begin.

I brush my teeth quickly and run a brush through my hair. Taking one long look into the mirror and smile. Opening the door to walk back to the bed I notice Jordan is already under the covers, shirtless, and a pair of black sweats peak from his V.

He is flipping through the channels on the tv and looks up at me. His eyes widen, "Remind me to thank your parents for arranging this set up." He smirks and I smile back innocently.

Slowly making my way to the bed, I turn around to put my phone on the nightstand and deliberately bend down where my thong is showing. When I turn around to pull the covers back, Jordan is closer to me with a fat grin on his face.

"Down boy." I joke climbing into bed and pulling my covers up.

"You sure have grown up." He says looking at me his eyes darkening.

"So have you." I inch towards him.

"Well lets have a little fun like old times." He slides a little farther into me. So close our legs touch.

I inch in closer. Our shoulders are close enough to touch and he ducks his head to lean into me some more when I bend around him and grab his pillow, smacking him on the side of the head, and putting it between us.

"What the hell, Mace?" He growls.

I laugh, "Your brain obviously never grew up with your body." I roll my eyes and grab the other pillow behind him making a wall inbetween us, "Don't mistake my beauty for stupidity, Smith." I tell him sternly and roll over to face the other way, making sure my ass and thong is out from the covers just enough to mess with him the rest of the night.

"You are a bitch." He scowls.

I turn off the light and lay my head down, "If being a bitch means I know how to set boundaries with assholes like you, then so be it."

Jordan Smith can have blue balls all night and I'll get my beauty sleep.

A win is a win.

Chapter Six
Jordan

The gym in the chalet is on the bottom floor and it's huge. Lined with workout machines that you would find in any commercial gym plus a sauna in the back. The floor to ceiling windows give a beautiful view of the Colorado mountains behind me. Thankfully, the snow is not falling yet this morning, but it lays on the top of the mountains like a white blanket from yesterdays downfall. So far, I have run five miles on the tread mill, done fifty pull ups, and an ab workout yet nothing is getting the picture of Macy's ass out of my head. My god, I have not had blue balls like that since high school. Ironically enough, she was the one who gave them to me then too. The woman infuriates me. How in the hell am I supposed to get through a week with her in the same bed as me while she teases me knowing good and damn well what it does to me.

I know she is playing me, and I honestly do not blame her. I deserve this kind of karma for what I did to her. For what I put her heart through. She did not deserve that, and my mistake made her move across the entire country from everyone she knew just to get away. If only she knew why I had to do it, she would forgive me. She does not know that it hurt me too. But it's not right for me to bring that up to her. It's water under the bridge and I'm proud of the damn she has built to keep herself alive. Life was not always nice to us as teenagers, but I made it a point, even if I had to stay behind and suffer for it, I was going to keep her safe.

"Damn man, think you are over doing it? We got a fun day planned with the wedding party; you might want to go shower that sweat off." Dylan's voice says coming from the doorway. I knew if anyone would find me down here it would be him.

I grumble, "Didn't sleep good last night man. Needed to get up and move around."

Dylan laughs, "Let me guess, Mace made you sleep on the floor?"

A fire ignites in my chest at hearing him call her Mace, "yes. Floor was rough." I reply short clipped.

Dylan smirks, "I told you; she has grown into a hell of a woman now. She will put even the cockiest Jordan Smith in his place." He turns to leave but turns back to say, "Never thought I'd see the day you two would be back in the same place again. She was determined to get away from you."

I'm gutted.

He chuckles, "Breakfast is served if you want to grab a bite before you shower. Paige's wedding planner has a full itinerary for us today." He leaves but I caught the eye roll about the itinerary just before he is out of sight.

I sigh, grabbing a towel from one of the benches, and use it to rub the sweat off my face. I'm already thinking of a way to get back at her for last night so before breakfast, I think I may just get a shower and make myself right at home.

Macy

I am pleased when I roll over to find the bed empty. It may have been against my morals, but I am thoroughly delighted it got me a win. As far as I am concerned, a win is a win when you out smart the cocky Jordan Smith.

I'm not naïve, I know he follows me on social media, and I would be lying if I said I did not follow him back. I keep up with what he's doing; I don't stalk him or anything, just curious from time to time. I saw what he did after we broke up, the girls he supposedly dated, the parties he went to, and the life he was living. It hurt me more watching him move on with his life like he never cared about me than anyone realized, so I tried to do the same. Although I went a different route; I did not date but I made friends. I did not go to parties but I did find myself immersed in beautiful stories about love and life. I would go out to eat with my girlfriends and would focus fully on my grades. If he did see me post that I was at a party, it was only to make sure he thought I was out being a slut and not thinking of him, which I was sitting on my couch most of the time binging my favorite shows. I told myself I would not come back home because it would only make the walls I built up come down faster.

Yet here I am sharing a bed with this fucker.

I pull the covers back and get up to find me a comfortable pair of sweatpants and pullover before treating myself to the kitchen for some breakfast.

Making my way into the kitchen, my sister, parents, Dylan, and some of the bridal party is already making their plates. There is food all over the kitchen island; pancakes, eggs, muffins, a variety of fruit, and juices for drinks.

"Sleep good honey?" My dad asks coming up to hug me.

"Yes I did!" I say happily.

"Jordan said you made him sleep on the floor last night." Dylan chimes in and I look at him confused for a moment.

"I didn-"I start but my mother butts in, "Oh Macy, do not make him do that. He can sleep in the bed just as much as you can." She comes up to hug me.

I huff, "Yeah okay mom. You are right."

Pulling out of her hug, I walk around the island, grab a plate, and put some pancakes and fruit on it. Reaching for a glass on the bar, I fill it up with some apple juice.

"Better hurry and eat." Paige says, "Mary is going to be here soon, and she has a big day planned for us."

I grumble, "Does the day include clothes I need to wear outdoors? If so, I need to go shopping." I laugh.

"Nah, go through my closet. Grab some jeans and a long sleeve shirt and jacket. She said we are going on a tour of the mountain side. You can wear a pair of my hiking boots"

"I'll eat this in my room." I gesture to my plate, "I need to go get ready."

Everyone smiles and waves me off as I walk back up the stairs and to my bedroom. I open the door to find that the room is still empty - Thank God.

Putting my breakfast down on the corner table in the room and open the door to the bathroom to brush my hair and teeth. As the door swings open, my mouth falls with it.

Jordan is standing in front of the vanity, brushing his teeth, fully naked.

His body is still dripping wet from the shower, his hair brushed back, and his muscles are — incredible. My mouth goes dry.

"Oh shoot. I forgot to lock the door." He grins at me after rinsing his mouth out.

"You are an asshole." The words leave my lips, but my eyes stay glued to his dick. I'm speechless.

"You could have joined me." Jordan says snapping me out of my trance.

"Ha." I laugh sarcastically, "You are so childish. I need the bathroom so hurry up. And next time, lock the damn door." I snarl at him and turn walking back into the bedroom to my breakfast plate.

"You asked for war last night, Mace." Jordan says as he enters the bedroom shirtless but thank God, he has pants on now.

"Be careful what you wish for, Smith." I grin, popping a grape in my mouth.

Chapter Seven
Macy

Paige's wedding planner is a woman around our mothers age who looks like she would be a Girl Scout leader as she hikes through the snow leading us to our destination. Her plan was for us to do team building skills today- *a wedding party who works well together helps the day go smooth together* – or whatever the hell she said.

Apparently, her name is Mary, and she pulled up this morning at the chalet in a white suburban that we all piled together in. Thankfully, the men all sat in the back and us women crowded in the front with Mary. My parents opted to stay back and have dinner ready for us when we returned, which made me wonder how long we are going to be out here in the fucking cold.

Her car pulled up to a large parking lot that looked deserted since we are the only car parked in it. A large sign caught my eye outside the car window – **Best Chair Lift of Colorado.** I know exactly where we are at, Paige and I use to come here as kids with our parents. There's a big pavilion at the top of the lift where you can see for miles. With a concession stand and a fire pit around with corn hole and games.

This won't be so bad.

We all pile out her suburban one at a time, waiting on her to tell us what to do next.

"Okay your first exercise for the day," Mary starts as she walks around to us, locking her car, "You are going to ride this chair lift to the top with your partner that is walking you down the aisle. Or meeting you at the end." She winks at Paige and Dylan.

I give my sister a death glare, "I am not riding in that lift with him."

"Mace, please." She gives me her best puppy dog eyes.

"If I remember correctly, he is afraid of heights." I whisper to her.

"Then its best that you are with him and not someone who doesn't know him well." She reassures me with a grin and walks off with Dylan to the first lift.

I stand back, watching as one by one, each bridesmaid and groomsman get in the lift together. Watching the last lift go up, I feel Jordans presence beside me. His face has fear written all over it.

"Okay, you two." Mary looks at Jordan and I gesturing to the lift; we are the only two left.

"Is there not another way?" I ask her.

"Only way up is together." She grins and pushes us towards the lift.

We stand on a line as the swing comes around for us to sit down on it, giving us no choice but to take our seats on the swing. The guy working the lift pulls down the safety bar over our body and says, "Have fun you two love birds."

"We ar-" I start but he turns and walks away from us not caring.

I look in-front of me as the platform goes away from under our feet and nothing is below us besides snow and trees. The view is breath taking. The snow looks like powder around us, and we are in the middle of a Christmas wonderland. This was my favorite thing as a kid, the magic in this time of the year. The magic of Christmas and all the magical feelings it holds. It felt like from the top of the lift you could see the North Pole itself.

"Jordan look" but when I look over at him, his knuckles are white as he grips the safety bar to death. His eyes are closed, and his lip is trembling. For a big broody male, he looks like a scared little boy right now.

I poke him and he jumps, his eyes fleeing open, "Macy, I swear to God, don't move."

I giggle, "Where is Cocky Jordan gone?"

"Truce, Mace? At least here. You know how much I hate heights." His voice is trembling.

I do remember.

Macy
16 years old

The October wind picks up as I take the last couple steps up the hill to the top of the ridge. I pull my jacket around me trying to get rid of my shiver and take some deep breaths to slow down my heart rate. I am not much of a hiker, but I needed to get out of the house for a while. Sometimes I like to walk up here and look out at the valley below where our small town sits and imagine what my future will be like.

Our small town of Opal, Colorado only has about two thousand people and from the almost top of the ridge I am on, I am shocked there is even that many. I like to sit up here and envision what the world is like outside of our small town, and if I will ever get a chance to see it. Sure, my parents are well off and my sister and I have never known struggle, but this little town is all I have known of; something in my gut is telling me there's more to life out there.

Reaching the top, I notice the sun is starting to set and I smile at the excitement of getting to see the moon and stars soon. If it's a full moon, it will light up the whole world down below. I stop mid stride, the rock I normally sit on to get the best view and do the best thinking, is not vacant. No, instead there is someone standing on it, and he is standing really close to the edge.

"Excuse me, what are you doing?" I ask the guy with his back towards me. He is in a black holy tshirt and shorts that look like they are too big for him. His shaggy hair is hanging low on his face; I'd bet he has not had a hair cut in a while.

I look down at his feet. His sneakers have holes in them that I notice his big toe is sticking out from the side. No socks on his feet even though it's cold out this evening.

He jumps at the sound of my voice.

"I'm sorry I didn't mean to startle you," I say walking closer to him, "But you are very close to the edge. Why don't you sit down before you fall?"

I'm so close I could reach out to grab him if he did fall but as I look around at his face, I notice he is crying.

"Stay back." He finally says through tears, "I'm afraid of heights." He explains.

I stop moving. Fear is running through my veins, unsure what he is about to do. The boy does not look much older than me. Though I don't remember seeing him at school, I'm sure I would have remembered him around town if I had saw him before.

I finally think of something to say, "If you are afraid of heights, then why are you standing so close to the edge of the ridge?" I ask.

He closes his eyes and tears fall down even more, as he opens them he answers me with a tremble in his voice, "B-bec-because no one will miss me if I'm gone. No one will notice. No one will cry for me. Might as well face my fear and end it all together."

He takes a shuffle forward with the tops of his toes now hanging over the rocks edge.

"No, lets not do that. What is your name?" I ask him.

He stares out in front of him then answers me, "Jordan."

"Hey, Jordan. I'm Macy! Do we go to school together?" I ask trying to keep his focus on my questions and not jumping to his death.

He shakes his head with more tears, "No. I just moved here. But he found us." He sniffles, "I'm tired of the beatings."

I look at him in shock, "The beatings? Jordan... Do your parents beat you?"

He nods but stays silent.

I grab his hand and jump up on the rock beside him. He startles for a moment, but finally his eyes leave the world in front of him, and they lock on mine.

"Wh-what are you doing?" He asks me.

"You are not alone anymore, Jordan. You do not have to face this world alone. Someone does care about you. Me." I give him a soft smile.

"I feel so alone." He tells me. A tear sits at the end of my eye.

"We are in this together. Let's just get off this rock first." I grin.

"Okay, Macy." He smiles stepping back from the ridge and off the rock still holding my hand. He helps me off the rock and pulls me into him. Before I know it his lips land on mine and he's kissing me. My first kiss with a stranger I just talked out from jumping to his death. This is not how I thought my night would go.

Present Day
Macy

We are almost at the top of the lift when it stops suddenly, letting those ahead of us have time to get off. The memory I just had of the ridge, has made my heart rate accelerate. That evening, on that ridge, changed my life in so many ways. It was the defining point to what the next few years would be like for me. I saved his life and he ruined mine by just a few short words.

Our feet dangle under us as the lift sways from the abrupt stopping and Jordan starts to panic. His face goes pale, and from his movement, the lift starts swinging more violently. His hands start to pull on the safety bar to lift it. Thinking quickly, I grab his forearm.

"Hey, hey. Jordan. Look at me." I tell him grabbing his face, so his eyes meet mine, "Look at my eyes, listen to the sound of my voice."

He takes deep breaths while his eyes are glued to mine.

"You are okay. You are going to be okay. We are in this together, remember?" I reassure him.

He starts to slowly calm down and his lips curl into a smile, "you remember?"

I give him a soft grin back, "I do. How could I forget, that was the night I got my first kiss." My cheeks blushed.

"You saved my life that night." Jordans voice sounded strangled.

"Funny how fast life changed." I mumble.

His eyes turn soft, "Macy, don't do that."

"It's true, Jordan. Life did change, drastically for us. Choices were made and life changed." The words leave my lips as the lift starts moving again and we top the entrance of the top of the ski lift.

But Jordans eyes stare into me; I turn forward. He stays silent but I can feel his gaze.

"You made it!" Paiges voice snaps Jordans eyes from me to the party waiting for us at the top.

"Thanks to Macy." Jordan smiles at me, but I keep my eyes away from him.

I cannot do this again.

Chapter Eight
Jordan
17 years old

Some people would say a shitty day consisted of spilling their coffee on their outfit, running late to be somewhere, or maybe oversleeping. Mine would be a lot worse than anyone else's combined.

My father never wanted me and don't worry, before you say, "That's not true, Jordan." I know it is because he told me daily. I was something that he did not care the slightest about. Normally dads hug their children, tell them they love them, and are around to watch them grow up. Not Allen Smith. His greatest joy was the high he got from the drugs he used and the beatings he put on my body.

He would be gone weeks at a time and boy did I enjoy those weeks where it was just my mom and I. I kept to myself most of the time and helped her around the house – she tried her hardest to keep us afloat.

Today was the day everything changed. Mom moved us a couple of cities away when she got her new job, and I was hopeful this meant he could not find us. Usually, he just wanted a quick fuck from her, some money, to beat me, and then he was gone again.

I am sitting at the dinner table eating supper when the front door flies open, and my father walks in. Mom jumps to her feet and runs to hug him. Why she always turns a blind eye, I will never understand. But me, I just keep eating my supper.

"You found us!" My mother says cheerfully to him, but I can see the fear in her eyes.

He gives my mother a kiss and drops his bags to the floor.

"Are you not going to give your father a proper greeting." His voice rings into the dining room.

"Hey, dad." I say emotionless but keep eating my food. I knew I was tempting the bear. I knew what I had coming but I was getting so tired of it. He would always win, he would always find us, and I had no one protecting me over it. I had already made up my mind that the day he finally came back home or found us, was the day I was going to do it.

He moves away from my mother's hug and stalks over to me, grabbing my plate and throwing it across the room. Food goes all over the wall and my mother gasps, "Allen, please don't."

"You will hush your mouth." He sternly orders my mother, and she shuts her lips.

"I am the man of this house, Jordan. When I speak or enter, you respect me. Is that understood?" He glares down at me but I don't look at him.

"Yes, sir." I finally mumble.

Slap.

His hand slaps me across the face and my mother starts to whimper, "Allen, please."

"I SAID HUSH!" He turns to my mother pointing at her and she goes silent again.

"I did not hear you, Boy." He exclaims.

I bring my eyes up to him, showing him I am not afraid, "Yes. Sir." I say sternly.

His hands go around my shirt collar and picks me up off the seat I'm in with ease looking me in the eyes, "Don't you go testing me now boy. I'll beat you to a crisp. I never wanted you anyway. It won't be no skin off my back." He throws me back down in the chair and walks away down the hall into the bedroom.

My mother rushes to me as he is out of sight and holds my face in her hands, "Jordan. Please stop testing him. He is going to hurt you."

I sigh, I wish she would stand up for me. For us.

"Mother, I'm going out for a little bit with some friends. I will be home later. Don't wait up for me." I give her a long and tight hug, "I love you."

"I love you too son. One day you will get out of this town and will do so many great things." Her voice breaks.

I sigh and nod. I don't want her to worry about me tonight, but I will not be coming back home.

No one cares about me, not even her. If she did, she would have protected me from that man long ago.

I grab my shoes by the front door and walk out, giving one last look to the home I will not be coming back to. I'm not really meeting friends, but she does not have to know that. I'm going to hike up to the ridge that looks over the valley the town is in. She will never suspect me going there; I'm afraid of heights.

Jordan
Present Day

Paige's wedding planner is an annoying woman. What happened to enjoying free meals and beer at wedding events? Now we are paired with the person we are going to be walking with to do trust exercises, in the fucking cold.

It's pure insanity. For my mental state and my balls.

I do get to spend my time with Macy though, so I guess we can call it a win.

I should be embarrassed about the chair lift reaction – and if it was anyone else with me, I probably would have tried to play it off. But I had Mace with me, and I'm thankful I did.

She talked me off those rocks so many years ago, but the hurt in her eyes when she said life changed drastically, tore at my heart a little. I knew I had hurt her, I knew there was no going back when I left her out of the blue that morning, but if she only knew why I did it. Why I had to leave her.

"Mr. Smith?" Mary, the annoying wedding planner, says and snaps me back to the crowd around us. Sometime between getting off the chair lift and now we are all sitting around a camp fire area together and everyone is starring at me.

"Yes?" I ask confused.

Mary chuckles, "Since you have been off in another world, how about you start first."

"Start what?" I ask looking around, noticing Macy is seated next to me.

She is grinning at me and my face turns red with embarrassment.

Mary huffs, "We are all going around and telling how we know the groom and bride to be."

"Oh," I shift in my seat, "Um," I clear my throat, "Paige and Dylan have been in my life since my teenager years. They are more than just friends at this point, they are family. Dylan and I became like brothers when I was sixteen," I give Dylan a knowing look and he nods with a grin, "I met Paige shortly after Dylan and I met. They dated all throughout high school. We were all really close growing up." My eyes shift to Macy who looks away quickly when my eyes meet hers.

"So sweet." Mary swoons, "Okay Macy, your turn."

I turn giving all my attention to Mace.

She starts, "Well, Paige is my big sister and the biggest pain in my ass." Everyone laughs and Paige rolls her eyes jokingly, "Her and Dylan dated all throughout high school, so it was like I had a big brother around too." She grins, "I knew they were meant to be, they were that couple that everyone wanted to be. You could tell they loved each other from the very beginning." She pauses and looks at me for a split second before looking back at the bride and groom, "Even Jordan and I had a bet going one time that we would be an aunt and uncle before they got married."

Everyone chuckles and Paige covers her face, "You did not have to tell everyone that." She hisses.

"I had forgot about that!" I laugh, "We had like one hundred dollars in on it. I remember you were so excited and thought we would be the best aunt and uncle!" Macy grabs my hand and squeezes it, hard.

I stop myself. It was not the pain of her squeezing that made me stop my sentence, it was the spark I felt when she touched me. I felt it on the chair lift, but I thought it was just my adrenaline. Her nails dig into me, and her eyes are as wide as saucers.

"Y'all would have been the best aunt and uncle though!" Paige smiles but then realizes what she just said and shakes her head, "Sorry."

Macy turns to her, her hand still holding mine, "It's okay. I will still be the best aunt someday." She winks at Paige.

Mary turns to Rylee asking her to share how she knows the bride and groom but their talking gradually is drowned out when I notice how upset Macy looks.

Macys eyes stare into me, "How dare you." She whispers.

"Macy, I'm sorry. I got caught in the moment." I state.

"You have not changed at all. Never thinking about anyone else but yourself" She says letting go of my hand and turning towards everyone else.

I can't focus on what anyone is saying anymore. All I can focus on is the hurt I saw in her eyes again. Same as the way they looked on the lift.

The not so Best Man

My heart rate climbs as the shame and guilt swallow me.

I am such a selfish prick bringing up a part of life that is no longer relevant no matter how much I wish it was.

Chapter Nine
Macy

My parents have a five-star catered dinner waiting on us in the dining room when we arrive back from our trip to the chair lift experience. Mary dropped us all off and explained that she would be back first thing in the morning for another fun filled day of *team building*!

Wonderful. – that was sarcasm. I still do not understand why my sister hired this crazy woman.

"Oh my goodness this looks wonderful, Daddy!" Paige exclaims to our father as we all enter the dining area. Our parents are standing at the entrance patiently waiting for our return. They both go into the kitchen to gather a few more plates for the table while we all try to find our seats.

Kelly, one of the bridesmaids, walks by me and whispers, "You lucky bitch. Getting to walk down the aisle with Jordan Smith AND share a room with him? I need you to enjoy it for all of us." She winks at me.

"Nah, he slept on the floor." I give her a soft smile and she looks at me puzzled.

"Girl. I would never." She laughs walking off to find a seat.

"Is there any assigned seating tonight?" I ask Paige and she shakes her head, no.

"Thought it would be nice for everyone to mingle where they wanted tonight." She smiles.

I let out a big puff of air from my lungs, I've been around Jordan enough today and I'll have to share the bedroom with him tonight, a little break would do my mind some good.

"Mind if I sit in between you two?" I ask Greg and Frank who both look surprised and intrigued at the same time while I gesture to the empty seat in between them.

The hair on the back of my neck pricks and I know by now, I must have Jordan's attention.

I Ignore the sensation and smile at the men before me, "go right ahead" Frank grins at me and I nod taking the seat in between him and Greg.

"What are you doing?" I hear Jordans voice behind me.

"What ever do you mean?" I ask batting my eyes with a grin.

He puts his hands on his hips like a teenage girl, "I thought you was suppose to be sitting beside me?" He ask confused.

"No, there is no assigned seating tonight. Thought it would be good to mingle with the other guests this evening since I was with you most of the day." I give a slight smile at the men sitting beside me and turn away from Jordan.

His hand goes to my shoulder, and I jump at the fire that surges though my skin, particularly making its way down inbetween my thighs.

"Macy, I would prefer you sit next to me." Jordans words seem slightly hoarse.

"Come on man. Leave some pussy for the rest of us. You have her in your bed at night. We can have her the rest of the time." Frank says and my mouth flies open appalled.

Before I am aware of what is going on, Jordan has picked him up out of his chair and pinned him up against the wall of the dining room. I jump out of my seat getting to them just in time before Jordan says, "If I ever hear you say anything disrespectful about Macy again, I will personally make sure you are rolling down the aisle Saturday in a wheel chair. Is that understood?" His eyes glare into Frank.

Frank nods, his whole body shaking with fear.

"Good." Jordan says letting Frank down, "Now, apologize to her."

My mouth seems to not be capable of closing as it hangs open, "Jordan, stop." I finally whisper.

"No, Macy. He said things about you that should have never been said. Now, he is going to apologize." Jordan looks at Frank sternly.

The whole room is quiet, staring at us.

"I-I'm sorry, Macy. It was a joke." Frank finally says.

"Oldest line in the book Frank. Be a man and stop making excuses." Jordan says.

Frank looks at me and says again, "I'm sorry Macy. It won't happen again."

I nod at Frank in acceptance of his apology and he quickly walks away back to the table.

Jordan's eyes meet mine and then turn to everyone else, "Sorry everyone. Just need to teach Frank a lesson. Now we can get back to a great dinner." He smiles and sits down beside Dylan who is eyeing him curiously. Obviously a little angered but I cannot tell if it's at Jordan or Frank.

Paige looks at me and I mouth, "What the fuck."

Our parents walk back into the kitchen and my mother looks my way, "Macy, take a seat honey. The food will be cold."

Other than the seat I was sitting in, the only other open seat is beside Jordan.

Perfect. – Again, sarcasm.

Chapter Ten
Macy

We all got through dinner with laughs and smiles, although I could feel the heat coming from Jordan sitting beside me. His right leg bounced like adrenaline just kept coursing through him with no where to go.

Where did that outburst towards Frank come from?

Sure, I've seen Jordan's protective side towards me, he once tried to bash Collin McGuire in the head with a baseball bat in gym class for calling me a slut. Everyone in the school talked about it for weeks after and no one dared to say anything about me again if Jordan was around.

Tonight's outburst was different. The tension in Jordan's body proved that to me. What it was though, I'm still trying to wrap my head around. The last time he even looked at me with any type of passionate emotion was the night he told me he loved me, and we would take on this world together. When he told me I was his forever and we made love that night.

That was another lifetime ago.

After dinner, everyone excused themselves to their rooms. Dylan and Paige were no where to be found so I figured they were in one of their rooms with the door locked. I told my parents goodnight and headed up the stairs, to change into some bedtime clothes and relax after this crazy day I have had.

Opening the door to my bedroom, I stop halfway as I enter when Jordans eyes meet mine. He is sitting on the edge of the bed, his hair is in a mess, and his sad eyes look back at me. I slowly make my way inside, shutting the door and gradually walking over to the bed sitting down beside him.

We both sit there staring straight at the wall for what felt like an eternity. I notice his leg is bouncing again like it did at dinner. I place my hand on his knee to steady it and I look at him, "Jordan…are you okay?"

He slowly turns his head from staring at the wall and he looks at me, for the first time since we were teenagers, I see tears in his eyes, "I don't know what is wrong with me."

I grab his arm and say, "What was that about tonight, with Frank"

He lets out a big breath, "No one talks to my Mace that way."

I let out a deep huff, "Jordan, I am a big girl. I can take care of myself. And I am not your Mace anymore."

He turns to me, "You should always be protected. You should always be took care of. I did you so wrong, Macy. Being back here, with you, memories are flooding my mind. I am so sorry."

His big brown eyes look at me full of hope, lust, desperation and then his lips meet mine. My eyes close as my body reacts to the familiarity of him. Sure he's a man now, every bit of him. But I remember him. That scared boy that was on that ridge, who became my best friend and first love. My hand goes to his chest and our kiss deepens, his tongue sweeps in massaging mine. Jordan's hands go to my waist and in an instant, I'm straddling him, rocking my hips back and forth over his dick. The tension making me moan into his mouth.

My eyes widen when I realize what I am doing and I push myself off him, creating space between us and slowing my breathing, "W-we can't do this." I gasp.

Jordan's now impressive bulge in his pants is all I can manage to look at and he grins at me, "Come on Mace. Our bodies remember each other well." He stands and walks over to me, puts his hands around my waist and starts pulling me towards him.

"Jordan," I sigh, "If you think you get forgiveness that easy from a few words, you are terribly mistaken." I push myself from him, walking towards the bathroom.

"Oh, come on Mace. You just going to leave me here with blue balls again?" Jordans voice says darkly.

I chuckle, "We did say this is war, didn't we?" And I give him an evil grin as I close the bathroom door behind me and lock it. Walking over to the bathroom vanity and look at myself in the mirror. My lips are bruised, my hair is a mess, cheeks flushed, and my chest red. The throbbing down in-between my thighs is getting more intense by the minute.

Turning on the shower, I undress and step inside. Desperate for some type of release, I hope the pressure in the shower head will be enough to take the throbbing away.

Jordan

Macy had no remorse for me as she walked off into the bathroom to take a shower. My dick throbs under my pants as I lay back on the bed listening to the shower water running. I had her in my arms for the first time in years and it was better than any fantasy I have had of her through the years.

This woman is driving me insane – mentally and physically.

My eyes widen and I sit straight up as I hear moaning coming from the bathroom. My body goes still as I listen again to see if I was mistaken.

Jordan.

A moan of my name comes from the bathroom and my cock throbs in my pants.

Is Macy in there getting herself off to the thought of me?

But the sounds coming from the shower are intoxicating. Blood rushes down my core in record speed and I get dizzy at the thought of what I'm hearing. She's in the shower, naked, pleasuring herself and moaning my name.

I lay back on the bed with my back against the headboard and unbutton my pants, letting my shaft spring out; my pre cum already making the head wet.

Jordan, please. Fuck me.

I hear Macy moan in the bathroom. Taking my dick in my hand, I pleasure myself to the sound of her moans. Those sweet, sweet moans making me imagine what it was like to be inside her. I picture her straddling me like before when she was kissing me. Instead, she is naked, and her breasts are bouncing in front of my face. My pumps get more erotic as her moans deepen in the next room and when I hear her release, so do I.

Coming down from my climax, I grab a tissue from the nightstand, wipe myself up with it and then button my pants back up. After a moment, the bedroom door slowly opens and Macy comes out, her hair wet, and dressed in silk nighttime pj's. I'm a little disappointed she didn't try the thong again tonight.

"Can I trust you to keep your hands to yourself without a pillow fort in between us?" She asks me with a side eye.

I smile, the little devil girl herself. She just got off to the thought of me; but yet, here she is playing a bitch again. I grin, "Maybe."

Her hands go to her hips and then she looks around, "What is that on the headboard?" She asks and my eyes widen.

Shit.

I turn to see what she is looking at and I notice it. Holy shit, I must have cum hard.

"What is that?" She ask again getting a closer look.

"I have no idea." I say trying to play it off.

Macy grabs a Kleenex from her side of the bed and wipes it off, throwing it in the trash.

"Whatever it was, it's gone now." She says without another thought, "Anyways, hands to yourself." She says pointing at me as she folds back the covers.

"Okay." I say rolling my eyes but secretly letting out a big breath once she climbs into bed and rolls over away from me.

This is going to be a hell of a week.

Chapter Eleven
Macy

I wake to the feeling of something large holding me down. No, wait, something warm and large that is…snoring?

I blink my blurry eyes a few times until the world around me comes into focus. The most annoying sound of snoring rings in my ears and I quickly realize who it is coming from…

"Jordan?" I whisper but the snoring continues.

It's impossible for me to move, this six foot alpha man that is cuddling me like his life depends on it. His leg is even wrapped around my bottom half.

I try my hardest not to giggle at the site before me.

"Jordan." I whisper a little louder and the snoring stops.

"Wake up sleeping beauty." I joke as his head nuzzles farther into me and his eyes flutter.

That's when I realize, he's hard.

His man hood is pressed so hard into my side from the cuddling that it feels like a tree branch is poking me.

"Jordan!" I yell and his eyes open wide.

"Oh, shit." He says backing away from me fast and I giggle.

"Still a cuddler, huh?" I joke.

"I do not cuddle." He says sternly sitting up on his side of the bed.

"Since when? You were always a cuddler." I joke again.

Jordan's eyes look at me, a little pain in them this time, "I have not cuddled anyone since you." He says leaving me alone as he goes into the bathroom, shutting the door behind him.

A weird emotion hits my chest. I push the covers off of me and head to the bathroom door. The knob turned – *he didn't lock it.* I push the door open seeing Jordan standing at the vanity looking at himself in the mirror.

"It's okay, Jordan. I was just joking." I laugh but my smile fades all together when I see the hurt still in his eyes as he turns to me, "It's not okay, Macy."

I sigh, "Oh sure it is. I do not hold it against you."

Jordan turns, walking to me. He gets so close, our noses almost touch. I gasp not knowing what he's about to do. His right hand goes to my ear and he tucks my hand behind it. Then he does something he use to do all the time when he wanted to reassure me he would always be here, he kissed my forehead; then he left the room. My brain misfires and my forehead tingles from his lips.

A memory from years ago takes over…

Macy
16 years old

Today was an odd day, Jordan was not answering any of my text messages and he did not make it to our spot we meet at on Wednesday afternoons for ice cream. I decided to walk the five blocks to his house to check on him before going home for the night. The trailer park he lived in was run down but I knew a few of the families that lived there from school so I was not afraid being out at dusk in the area.

I had never been to Jordan's home, but he had told me where it was. I looked through the mailboxes until I found one with the last name, Smith, on it. The trailer was smaller than a double wide and had a small porch attached to the front with dead flowers in the pots that lined the steps. With each step I got close to the front door, and I could hear people inside. They were yelling.

I debated on knocking on the screen door as I heard something that sounded like glass break inside the trailer. But then I saw him. Through the plastic screen on the door, I saw a man pick Jordan up by his shirt and sling him through the house. Jordan's back hit the wall with a thud. He looked almost lifeless.

Knocking was not on my list anymore. I grabbed the handle of the door and flung it open running inside and grabbing the man who had hurt Jordan. Jumping on his back, I hit him over and over again.

"What the hell. Get this little bitch off me." The man yelled but I held on for dear life.

"Macy! No!" Jordan screamed at me in fear.

The man walked as fast as he could backwards into the wall, making me scream out in pain as I let go and fell off of him. "Friend of yours?" The man asked Jordan as he ran to help me up.

"Dad, Leave her alone." Jordan asked hoarsely as he helped me to my feet.

"Such a beautiful girl." The man says to me with a grin and he steps towards me. Jordan's protective hand goes around my waist.

"Is this your girlfriend?" Jordan's dad asked bringing his hand to my chin and lifting it.

"Don't you fucking touch her." Jordan ordered sternly.

His father moved his fingers from my chin, down my neck, over my chest and circled each breast, running them farther down until he touched my stomach, "If my son won't put you to use, I can." His dad smirks at me and I snarl, "Fuck you."

He chuckles grabbing my hair and pulling me to him, "I'll gladly fuck you."

Jordan grabs the closest thing to him- a baseball bat and swings right at his dads head while he's focused on me. The big bear of a man falls to the ground unconscious and Jordan grabs my hand pulling me out of the house.

I am not sure where we are when Jordan finally stops running. His hand still holding mine and by now we are both out of breath. He stops and looks me over, "Are you okay, Mace?" He asks concerned.

I nod, holding back tears, finally coming down from shock, "I-I came looking for you. I was worried."

Jordan held my head in his hands and tears swelled in his eyes, "I love you for that but please do not worry about me. Please never put yourself in harms way again – even if it is for me."

I look at him as a tear slides down my cheek, "for you, I will always put myself in harms way. I'll always be here for you." I smile.

He kisses me tenderly on the lips, as he pulls back he says, "You and me, forever." Then he kisses my forehead.

"What was that for?" I ask.

"Anytime I kiss you on the forehead, it's me saying to you that I'll always be here." He grabs my hand in his staring off at the world around us but my eyes are already on my world-him.

Chapter Twelve
Jordan

How did the hell did I end up cuddling Macy last night?

The thought ringing in my head has me busting out of our bedroom door and downstairs to the kitchen. It's early and most of the house is still asleep – thank God.

I must have rolled over in the night and snuggled up to her. Something we both used to do when we would spend the night together. I guess subconsciously my mind knew where it wanted to be, in her arms.

My heart was hers. It has always been hers. Cuddling was part of intimacy I only wanted with her. If I could not have her, even if it was against my will, then I did not want those kind of feelings or memories with anyone else. I wanted to keep hers.

But why the fuck did I cuddle her like she was my own personal pillow.

Me coming to this wedding was only because of one reason- the text message I received. I was here to protect her. That's all. Too much is at stake right now for my heart to get in the way.

Entering the kitchen, I grab a glass from the cabinet and orange juice from the fridge.

"You are up early." Paige's voice enters the kitchen and I jump, "Your sister is a ray of sunshine in the morning." I snarl trying to play off my jumpiness.

Paige laughs and pulls a glass down grabbing the orange juice I had left on the counter, "I lived with her. You're not telling me anything I don't know." She pours her juice and we are both quiet for a minute then Paige says, "Thank you for sticking up for her last night. I always know when you are around, no matter what you two are fighting about, you will protect her." An odd emotion stirs in my chest while Paige finishes her drink, her hand goes to my shoulder as she exits the kitchen, "She was a lost puppy without you, Jordan. The good, bad, and all the things in between meant a lot to her. All I know is when you broke her heart, it was enough to make her move across the country from everyone. Please be gentle with her. She has come so far, and I would hate to see that ruined. She deserves the world."

I let Paige get almost out of the kitchen before I reply, "I know she does." But I caught the small grin from her as she exits.

Finishing my orange juice in silence, I look out from the windows in the kitchen. Colorado is a beautiful place, it almost seems unreal that I call it home. A grumble comes from the kitchen bar. I turn to find Brian, Macy's father, standing and watching me.

"Morning, sir." I nod.
"Jordan." He nods back.

He moves around the counter and walks over to the cabinet grabbing a coffee mug and fills up his cup with coffee that has already been brewed. I guess more people are up than I realized.

"My girl keeping you straight?" He asks finally after fixing his coffee mug.

I nod, "Yes sir. She has."

He grins, "Good." After a moment, he sighs, "Listen son, I know I don't like nor do I understand why things happened like they did between you and Macy years ago. But I just want you to know how proud Kristina and I are of you. Finishing your degree and getting that engineering job. I hope you know you have people in your corner here."

A tear forms in my eyes, this man has always looked after me, "Thank you, sir. You both have been so good to me through the years. I would like to pay you back some money for all the years you took me in."

He shakes his head, no, and smiles, "Take care of my girl, Jordan. Dylan told me what happened last night at dinner. I appreciate you standing up for her. I know you still love her. Whether you two get your second chance or not, I know you will do right by her either way." He pauses, "Just keep your junk in your pants." He raises an eyebrow at me.

I chuckle, "Yes sir."

What I really wanted to say was, *"Your daughter has given me blue balls for the past two nights so I do not see that being an issue."*

Chapter Thirteen
Macy

Mary has the whole wedding party on another wild adventure today. Four days before the wedding and we are hiking through the mountains of Colorado. Did I mention I did not pack clothes for these types of adventures? It's fucking December. I do not know what my sister is paying for this crazy Girl Scout lady who calls herself a wedding planner, but I feel like she needs to get a refund.

"Are there bears out here?" Paige asks Mary while we all get out of her suburban.

All of us stare at her with the same question and fear.

She giggles, "To answer your question, yes there is. But they are more afraid of you than you are them." She waves us off like we are naïve children.

"I don't think I hired you to take us through bear country." Paige snarled.

Dylan gives her a look of – please calm down.

I giggle, "I mean she has a point." Backing up my sister.

Mary looks at us seriously, "My dear, this is team building. If your wedding party does not get along, your day will fall to pieces." She points to Jordan and I, "Im talking to you two, obviously." I give her an evil glare while Paige giggles.

Mary pops the trunk of her SUV and tells us women to grab a backpack for each of us. Once we all have our backpacks secured she claps her hands, "Come! We have a schedule to keep. Those packs have food and water in them for the hike."

We all huff but follow the crazy woman onto the trail.

Following behind her, the men stay behind all of us ladies; I guess they think we will protect them from bears. We eventually all huddle around a sign of a map with the area laid out before us.

Mary turns to us, "Okay, partner up. Best Man and Maid of Honor, Bride and Groom, and Bridesmaid and groomsmen you are walking down the aisle with." She claps her hands wanting us to chop to it.

I roll my eyes at my sister who mouths with a grin, "Sorry."

Jordan, who has been quiet most of the way here, slowly makes his way over to me and stands beside me with out a word. *Odd.*

Everyone else gets with their partner and Mary goes around handing all of us tiny versions of the big map, "This is the area we are going to be hiking. Y'all notice on the map I have it marked with checkpoints. Each checkpoint has a key. Each key will open a box at your next check point and so on.

At the end there will be a giant box with a surprise for the winner the key will open. This terrain is not easy, take your time and do not rush. Help each other, talk about life, get to know one another. You have to finish this hike together or you forfeit."

I look around at everyone and at the map, it's large. I ask, "How long do we have to get to the finish line?"

"As long as it takes." She grins and walks back to her car.

"Wait. Where are you going?" Elizabeth, one of the bridesmaids, asks.

"To the finish line to wait on you." She puts her sunglasses on and leaves us.

I turn to my sister who stands in shock, "Paige. Please tell me she is kidding."

Paige is silent for a moment and finally says, "Well, be thankful you borrowed my shoes." She grins walking off with Dylan and the others onto the trail, each one taking a different route than the other.

I turn to Jordan who is still being oddly quiet, "Well, you ready?"

"Do I have a choice?" He finally says.

"Not if I don't either." I answer and open the map while walking towards our trail.

Colorado is beautiful and full of wildlife. Thankfully the snow has melted some since we have been here giving us an advantage of seeing the trail before us. We are a few feet higher in elevation than we were at the chalet and half of me guesses that is why Jordan is being so quiet. He has not said much to me while I lead the way looking at the map. His footsteps are the only reason I know he is behind me still.

"You okay back there?" I ask him after a few minutes of silence.

I look back for a moment while my feet keep moving and notice his hands are in his pockets, his head hangs low, and his feet are not making as big of a stride as usual.

I stop, allowing him some time to catch up to me and when he gets close enough, I grab his forearm and make him look at me, saying, "Jordan, what is the matter with you?"

"I just hate heights." He finally says, "And the fact that this was suppose to be a fun week and I have had no fun the entire time I've been here. Just blue balls."

I giggle, "I'm sure one of the bridesmaids wouldn't mind helping with that."

As soon as the words left my mouth, I regret them. No way in hell would I be okay with him sleeping with one of them, even if he isn't sleeping with me.

What is wrong with me?

The thought is gone within seconds as I clash into a hard surface, Jordan. Somehow, he has moved around me, and his chest has collided with mine. His nostrils flare above me as his eyes meet mine, "Let's make one thing clear, Mace. I do not care for any of those women."

My mouth gaps open but I am too stunned to speak. Jordan's hand goes to my chin, his thumb running across my bottom lip and his Adam's Apple slowly rises and falls, "The only one on my menu this week is the Maid of Honor, and she is being a pain in my ass." He smirks, letting go of my chin, grabbing the map out of my hand and walking off continuing down the trail. My feet neglect to move. My mouth cannot seem to close, and my mind is nothing but jelly. *What just happened?*

"Lets go this way!" Jordan states, snapping me out of my trance, my feet finally coming to life as I jog to catch up with him.

"Why that way?" I ask catching up to his side.

He looks at me with a smile, "Just feels right."

I smile back, weary of the underlying meaning of his word. He was always one who did those things. His worlds always had secret meanings.

The trail we turn off onto is smaller than the one we were just on. To me, it looked like it was made for bikes more than hiking. There's a little bit of an incline as we ascended up and Jordan grabbed my hand to help me as I climbed. The trail before us flattened as we reached the top and a creek flowed out before us with a small bridge on it. It looks damn near majestic.

"Oh this is beautiful." I squealed walking towards the bridge. "Jordan loo-"

Snap. I hear the camera from his phone snap a photo. I laugh, "What are you doing?"

"Just remembering this moment." He grins and puts his phone back in his pocket.

"Would you look at that," Jordan says as he joins me on the bridge pointing at the creek below, fish of all sizes swam below us, "I bet bears love this spot."

I snap my head at him, "I thought Mary was kidding about the bears."

He laughs at my naiveness, "Everyone knows there are grizzlies in Colorado, Macy. You've lived here your whole life. Do not be stupid."

My head is now on a swivel as I scan the area around us. Jordan laughs, walking around me to the end of the bridge, "Someone's been in the big city for too long." He laughs, "Their more scared of you than you are them. Besides, the chances of us seeing one is astronomical. If we do see one, I'm going to play the lottery as soon as we get back into town." He continues to chuckle as he leaves me on the bridge, getting back on the trail.

Catching up to him, the fear of seeing a bear finally declines and my steps are making strides with his. The creek flows beside us as the trail weaves and flows beside it. Rounding a curve up ahead, I freeze and grab Jordan's shirt, stopping him as his eyes were glued to the fish in the creek. I fall to the ground, and he lands on top of me.

"Jordan, get down." I order sternly as I crouch down beside a big rock beside me. The idiot stands back up thinking I am being funny.

"Macy, if you wanted to do the nasty, all you had to do was ask. Not jerk me on the dirty ground." He gives me a flirty grin as he wipes the dirt off his pants.

"Jordan, I swear to God, get your ass down here." I whisper harshly.

"Begging for it are we?" He pulls his jacket off and then starts to pull his shirt off but I grab his arm stopping him.

"Okay, now you are just giving mixed signals." He pouts turning back to the trail.

As soon as his eyes see what I have been trying to tell him, they widen.

A grizzly bear is standing up a few yards ahead near the creek, looking for its next meal.

The biggest and highest girly scream comes out of this alpha man beside me. He sounds like a five year old girl. But that's not even the worst part, once the scream ends, he faints.

The bear is not impressed by his dramatics at all, and neither am I. It stares at us for a moment and then walks off into the woods.

Seriously, it was not impressed at all at encountering us humans.

Watching it walk off, I finally ease myself up from behind the rock and kneel down beside Jordan, who's eyes are finally fluttering as he comes to, "What happened to 'They are more scared of us?' I did not see her fainting from fear." I giggle and he snarls.

Sitting up slowly, I hand him a water bottle from my backpack. He takes a few sips from it before giving it back to me, saying, "I need to go play the lottery."

I chuckle, "You need to get up off this ground first. You have mud and dirt all over you."

Putting my hand out, I help him up and we continue on our trial.

"By the way," I start, "What the hell was that scream?"

The look I'm given in response tells me to take my smirk off my face immediately.

But I don't.

Chapter Fourteen
Jordan

"We are lost, Jordan." Macy's words ring beside me as we continue along the trail. Ignoring her, scanning my eyes over the map, it doesn't make sense, we should be at the first checkpoint. It should be right in front of us, but it's nothing but trees and more trees. I swear we have been walking in circles this whole time. I know for a fact, I just saw that same bird shit on that rock we just passed a few minutes ago.

We have been out here for hours now and our water bottle is running low. My feet hurt and my balls seem to keep getting bluer the longer I'm out here with this woman.

Macy's eyes look at me with worry, "Jordan, I'm telling you we are lost."

"No we are no-…" my voice echoes as I fall. I'm tumbling down the side of the mountain we are on after I accidentally stepped off the side of the cliff that I did not even realize we were on. Thankfully, some of the terrain levels out and it stops me from falling to my death.

Catching my breath, I stop as laughter takes over my ears.

Is she laughing at me?

Looking up at the cliff I just tumbled down, Macy's hand is holding on to a tree as she's bent over horse laughing at the situation.

I huff, "Thanks for caring."

She starts to walk down the incline I just fell down.

"Whoa, wait. What are you doing?" I ask her almost hysterical, "You need to stay up there."

When she reaches me, still laughing, she grabs my chin and turns it behind me.

My eyes widen.

Those assholes.

The chalet is just a few yards away and Paige is standing on the balcony of the patio with a camera, Dylan is hysterically laughing, and the entire bridal party plus the wedding planner are all smirking. Embarrassment runs all over me.

"You fuckers did this on purpose." I snarl.

Macy puts her hand on her hip, "Please do not tell me that's true."

Paige's laughing subsides and she wipes a tear from her eye, "Oh it was a harmless prank. I needed you two to get along and I knew the only way that would happen was if you had to work together. The chair lift seemed to work but then this morning in the kitchen, Jordan still seemed a little irritated, so I needed to take it more extreme. The trail you were on just made a big circle. You two have been walking the same route for hours."

Paige looks so proud of herself.

"We saw a bear we could have died!" Macy squeals at her sister.

"No," Paige grins again, "You saw Dylan in a bear costume. Worth every penny I spent on it too seeing the go pro video of Jordan fainting."

"I'm going to kill you!" Jordan's voice snarls at Dylan who is waving a go pro in his hand.

"Sorry, man. It was too good to pass up. Never thought you would faint though." He laughs. "Although we need to talk about the stripping you almost did before it."

Macy's face goes red.

Paige ignores Dylan's comment and looks my way, "You guys look terrible. Go shower and freshen up. We are ordering pizza tonight."

While everyone retreats back inside the house, I turn to Macy whose cheeks are still flushed with redness. She looks down at her body and makes a displeased face, "Ugh. I smell like sweat and woods. I call dibs first!" She grins at me and takes off running down the hill towards the house.

Jumping to my feet, I race after her towards the house but held off my stride on purpose letting her think she won getting to the door first. As soon as we step inside, I look around for anyone who might see us and when the coast is clear, I grab her waist, spin her around, and lift her over my shoulder, taking her to our room. She squeals playfully the entire time as we reach the door. Kicking it open with my foot and closing it soon as we enter, I lock the door and take us both in the bathroom.

"What are you doing?" She asks me hesitantly while I put her feet down on the floor, close the bathroom door behind us, and lock it.

"Something I've been wanting to do since the moment you walked into this chalet." I state as I stalk to her, grab her waist with my hands, and pull her into me. My lips crash onto her's and at first, she thinks about fighting me, but almost instantly, her body relaxes, giving in and kissing me back deeper this time.

Lifting her shirt over her head, I throw it to the floor and my lips claim her neck, kissing and sucking while her tiny moans echo sweet hymns through my ears making the blood in my brain rush to my cock, causing it to throb and make me a little dizzy. Macy grabs the bottom of my shirt and lifts it over my head, my breaths becoming more erotic watching her eyes glisten over my muscles.

"Pants off." She orders and I smile.

"When did you get so bossy?" I smirk, unbuttoning my jeans while obeying her orders.

"Now your pants, ma'am." I command.

She backs up, slowly unbuttons her jeans, and slides them down her ass, thighs, and eventually steps out of them as they lay on the floor.

Macy

Never say never, because I am betraying every thought I had when I arrived here allowing this man to touch me like this. My body remembers him as it reacts to each touch, each kiss, each breath. This is the Jordan I missed.

We both step into the shower, completely naked, and Jordan turns the shower head on, allowing me to stand under it as my hair gets completely soaked. Mud and dirt fall to the floor, slowly making its way down the drain. Jordan's hand goes to my waist, pulling me into his chest while his – rather large - erection pokes me in the back.

I close my eyes as I feel his breath on my ear, "You are so beautiful, Mace."

I turn to face him, my breasts touching his chest, and instead of saying a word, I kiss him. His tongue parts my lips as it slides past them and it was like my tongue remembered him instantly. This man was my first love, I knew there was no way I could fully forget his touch.

He guides my back to the wall and picks up my right leg hanging it on his hip. His hand following the inside of my leg, up my thigh, and stops right before my folds. My breath hitches as he slowly runs his fingers over my sensitive area and I can feel the wetness on his fingers, he smirks while he kisses me.

"She's ready to play." He smiles into my lips and plunges two fingers into me without warning. My mouth flies open in an O shape as he thrusts them in and out of me, the sound of my wetness making the sweetest noise.

Taking his fingers from me, he lifts them up to my mouth and presses them to my lips, "You know what to do." He grins and I suck my arousal off his fingers. His eyes turn to flames as he watches.

He kisses my forehead right before he lines the tip of his dick at my entrance. We both watch as his dick enters me and both let out shaky breaths together right before his lips crash back down to mine. He is not rough, but he is not soft either with each thrust, my moans grow.

"You. Are. Perfect." Jordan says as he rocks in and out of me with so much passion. His movements feel like he's trying to savor and enjoy them. Like it's the air he needed to keep breathing.

My lips go to his neck, and I suck. My core tightens with tingles and his thumb goes over my clit, massaging it as he continues to drive rapidly in me, and I bite down on his shoulder as my orgasmn explodes all around him. The pulsing from my muscles make him climax with me.

I lay my head on his shoulder, coming down from the euphoria and trying to calm my breathing. It feels like he is doing the same thing. Shortly after our breathing slows, Jordan does something he should not have done, he leans back and kisses my forehead and that makes an emotion swell in my chest.

I can feel my walls coming down. The one I worked too hard to build up.

A memory floods me:

Macy & Jordan
16 & 17 years old

"Are you sure your parents are gone?" Jordan asks me as he slowly walks though the threshold of my parents house.

They are gone this weekend on a trip just them for their anniversary. So Paige and I have this house all to ourselves. Of course she invited Dylan over and I told Jordan to come over. He told his mom he was staying at Dylan's so she would not worry about him.

I laugh, "Yes, Jordan. They won't be back until Sunday! Come on, you can throw your bag down in my bedroom."

He follows me up the stairs to where my bedroom door sat open revealing my bed made with fresh white sheets and all my girly things. My room is a light cream color with a dark color bed frame and furniture. Jordan takes a look around, almost timid to walk in. He slowly walks in, taking in his surrounding and he turns to me.

"Your bed is huge." He finally says.

"I mean, I guess so. It's just a queen. Paige got to have a king because she is older." I shrug my shoulders. I've never been in his bedroom in his house so I do not even know what it is like.

Finally I ask, "What kind of bed do you have?"

His eyes hit the floor for a moment and then he answers, "Um, I don't. Mom does not make enough for luxury's like that. I sleep on the couch or I have a cot I pull out sometimes."

My eyes widen, "Oh, I'm sorry. I didn't know."

He shrugs, "Mom makes ends meet. She makes sure we have food, most of the time. And our bills are paid, even if they are late sometimes. But she does well for what she has. Allen does not give us money, it is all mom and sometimes she has to give him money for his drugs."

I nod, but stay silent. How do you respond to something like that when this life I live is all I have known.

"Okay you can a say it" I finally tell him.

"Say what?" He looks at me confused.

"That I'm an entitled bitch who doesn't know struggle." I smile at him.

"The fact that you open your home and life to me means you are far from an entitled bitch, Mace." He winks at me.

We just stand there in silence smiling.

"When is Paige and Dylan getting here?" He asks me as he puts his bag down on the floor by my bed.

"They were stopping to get pizza as soon as she meets Dylan after he gets off work and then coming over." I smile at him sitting on the edge of my bed.

He looks at me unsure what to do.

"What is wrong with you?" I ask him.

He rubs his hands through his hair, "I just have never spent the night with a girl before." He gives me a boyish grin walking over to the bed and slowly sitting down beside me.

"I'm not just your friend," I grin, giving him a soft kiss on the lips, "I am your girlfriend."

He kisses me back softly pulling back with a grin, "That still sounds so surreal. How lucky am I."

I snicker, "You are one lucky bastard that is for sure."

***

We have ate pizza, swam in our parents pool, and laughed until we cried this evening. The evening is coming to an end while the end credits roll ending the movie we just sat down and watched together.

"Well," Dylan says, standing up and holding his hand out to Paige, "It's time for bed." He winks at my sister and pulls her to her feet after her hand meets his. She laughs and grins at me, "You guys okay if we head on to bed?"

I laugh, "Yes. Goodnight you two. Love y'all."

They both say their good nights too and leave Jordan and I in the living room together.

Jordan's arm is draped around me since my head was laid over on him during most of the movie. I turn my head up at him and he kisses my forehead softly.

"I'm nervous." He whispers after his lips leave my skin.

I look at him confused, "Why?"

"Because Mace, you are out of my league. I do not deserve you and I don't want to mess this up." He states removing his arm from around me.

I stand up, turning the tv off, and hold my hand out for him to take it. When he finally does, after a moment of *contemplation, I turn going up the stairs to my room; turning the lights off to the first floor in the process.*

Entering my room, I close the door behind us and Jordan opens his bag of clothes.

"I'm going to change into some sleep clothes." He tells me.

I nod, taking the opportunity while he changes to change my clothes too.

The door to my bathroom closes and I hear the door lock. Walking over to my dresser, I take out some shorts and a tshirt to sleep in. Unclasping my bra, I slide it off and hang it on the knob of my dresser for in the morning. Throwing my dirty clothes into the hamper by my bathroom door, I quickly change into my new clothes and crawl into bed, grabbing the tv remote and pulling up the channels.

The bathroom door unlocks and Jordan comes out carrying his dirty clothes in hand while wearing some black sweat pants and a tshirt that I noticed had holes in it.

"You can throw your old clothes in the hamper. I'll do a load of laundry tomorrow." I told him.

He nods, putting his clothes down in the hamper with mine.

"Our washer and dryer stopped working last week. I have to go to the laundry mat to do our laundry when we need it done." He says nonchalantly, rounding the corner of the bed to the side I'm not on.

My heart constricts. I've never known a life like he has had to live. It makes me feel so embarrassed that those things I've never had to worry about.

"Bring them to me from now on until your washer and dryer is fixed. You can do them here, or I can. My parents won't mind." I assure him.

"No, I cannot do that to you." He tells me, shaking his head.

"But I'm offering, Jordan. Please don't use the laundry mat in town. It's dangerous out there at night anyways. Just bring them here." I smile at him.

He just looks back at me with an emotion in his eyes I cannot really put my finger on. It makes my heart skip a few beats though.

Jordan slides in on his side of the bed and pulls his covers up to his waist.

His body's warmth feels like home here beside me.

I think I'm starting to fall in love with him.

I slide over to him, his arm goes around me, allowing me to mold to his side placing my head on his chest. His heartbeat is like a hymn to my ears.

"Do you know what it's saying?" He asks me.

"No? What?" I ask.

"Every beat my heart is saying, Macy. Macy. Macy." He whispers.

I turn my head up so my eyes meet his, tears glistening in the corners, and I tell him, "Mine does the same for you, Jordan."

His lips crash onto mine − tonight is the night I lose my virginity to the first guy I ever fell in love with.

Chapter Fifteen
Macy

The morning sun is creeping through the window, and I am laying in his arms again. A place I never thought I'd be. I can feel his strong muscles wrapped around me and for the first time in a long time, I feel like I am where I belong. For so long, I ached for his touch, his protection, his love. I cried so many tears praying, begging, screaming for him to come back to me. The way he left me, came out of no where. One day we were talking about forever and the next he is telling me to go on with life without him. He was all I knew, and it wounded me in all the ways I never knew my heart could be wounded. He took a piece of me with him the day he left me; I wanted it back for the longest time no matter the consequences.

But is it enough to forgive him for what he did. Is it enough to look past all the years of hurt and anger. For so long I have run from the hurt and in a moment's time, I let him back in. I let the walls fall down with the slightest touch. Walls that took me years to build when I thought it would kill me.

Something pulls me out of my deep thoughts when I feel my rib cage being attacked. Jordan is on top of me, tickling me as I scream under him.

"Jordan!!" I scream and giggle trying to get out from under him, "Stop!!"

"Someone was thinking herself to death," he kisses my forehead, "I needed to get you to stop."

I swat my hand at him, "How did you know?"

He rolls his eyes as he sits his back up against the headboard of the bed, "Please Mace, at one point in time, I knew your thoughts before you even voiced them."

I smile, he did.

He was once the person I bared my soul to.

Our silence falls over the room for a moment, my hand goes to his chest, and my eyes meet his, I ask, "Why did you do it?"

Jordans eyes cloud with sadness. He kisses my forehead and pulls me into him, "I wish I could tell you."

I look at him confused as a loud knock hits our bedroom door startling us, "Wake up you two! We have things to do!" Paige's voice rings on the other end.

I roll my eyes and scoot out from under Jordan, "Duty calls." I laugh.

***

"Before rehearsal tomorrow night, we are going to do one more team building exercise!"

Mary's voice rings through the patio on the back porch of the chalet. Jordan and I got up and dressed for the day and decided to keep what happened last night to ourselves.

How would we explain it anyways.

I am not even sure what it means.

"So what's the plan?" Greg asks, standing around the other groomsmen and we all nod in agreement wanting to know the same.

"Well, today is going to be a little different..." Mary smiles as she grabs a few stacks of papers from her bag and hands us each one of them.

BEST ESCAPE ROOM OF COLORADO

I laugh turning to my sister, "One of your plans to keep me and Jordan from hating each other?"

She smirks, "Nope, not this one. This was all Mary's idea for all of us."

"Yes, it was my idea." Mary says with a smile. "You are all going to have to work together to get through the escape room in time. It is such a good team building exercise and this one is Christmas themed!!" She looks so proud of herself.

"Oh this will be so much fun!" Paige says excitedly, squeezing Dylan's arm.

Jordan slides in behind me and whispers in my ear, "Fun indeed."

Heat fills my core at his seductive tone.

"You guys will have so much fun!" My mom says as she comes in the room beside me. She looks over at me smiling, "You sure are glowing this morning."

"Mom, not now." I clip.

She winks at me and then turns to everyone else, "Lunch will be ready when you all come back. Brian is laying out steaks as we speak!"

***

Jordan

I do not understand why Mary has us all ride in her SUV every time we go somewhere together but all of us guys are basically all sitting on top of one another in the back seat. Dylan is going on and on about some big deal he has made at work and the other guys are listening with such intent.

Besides me. My focus is one thousand percent on my Mace. When she stopped thinking long enough to let me touch her last night, without fighting, it felt like I was back where I belonged. The place I have been missing for so long. When she asked me why I did what I did all those years ago, a rush of air left my lungs when the knock on the door interrupted us.

Because I know when I tell her the truth, she won't look at me the same.

There are just things I cannot change, and I made my choice.

I knew the choice I made would hurt us, but I had to protect her.

It was the only choice to keep her safe.

But God, I have missed her everyday since. She took a piece of my heart with her that day.

One of the bridesmaids said something funny and Macy's laugh rings like hymns through my heart. I actually felt it flutter. Her smile could always make me feel the biggest emotions – but her laughter, it did far more than just give me emotions. It felt like home.

I think she could sense me staring because for a brief moment, her eyes turn and meet mine. They twinkle in the way they always did when we would look at one another without being side by side; the look of our souls was always connected.

It's selfish of me, but I plan to soak up every moment I can with her while I am here. Once the wedding is over, no one can know we have been together.

I have to keep her safe.

Even if it means keeping her at arms length.

She is going to hate me, and I am fully prepared for it.

She can hate me as long as she is alive and protected.

The memories with her is what has kept me alive this far and it is what will keep me going even when I have to watch her move on with her life again, without me.

Jordan
17 years old

I cannot remember when the last time I laid down for bed not having to worry about when my next beating would be; if my father were going to walk through the house and lay into me again. I got to spend all day with Macy, Paige, and Dylan. We swam in Paige and Macy's parents pool, ate take out, and just enjoyed the rest of the summer we had.

I am about to start my senior year of high school and the thoughts of it being my last year in the school with Macy hurts to say the least. There has not been a day that's went by since she pulled my father off of me that I have not spent with her.

This girl saved my life.

I am a virgin and I know Macy is too. I've wanted nothing more than to give my virginity to her. Tonight, I had planned to do just that, but I would be lying if I said I was not nervous. This girl is everything I have ever dreamed of having. I grew up knowing I did not want the kind of relationship my parents have. I wanted a home, a wife, and kids I adored. I wanted to be in love with a woman who loved me back just the same. And even at 17 years old I believe I have found that in Macy.

She is the light in the darkness for me. The one I can always count on. The one I gave my heart to on that ridge that night even before I realized it myself.

"What is the matter?" Macy asks pulling out of our kiss as we lay on her bed.

"I just don't want to mess this up." I admit to her.

She smiles, "Jordan, you aren't. I want this. I want this with you."

"I love you, Macy." My voice says in almost a whisper.

She grins, "I love you, Jordan."

Our lips crash back onto one another, and that night was the night I gave everything to the girl who owns my heart.

Jordan

"Earth to Jordan." Dylan's waving his hands in front of me as the memory fades.

I focus my eyes on him, confused, "Yeah?"

He laughs, "Why were you staring at Macy so intensely?"

"I didn't realize I was." I try to play it off, "Honestly I'm not even sure what I was zoned out on. A memory or something." I try to sound confident.

Dylan pats my shoulder as the other guys continue with their own conversations, "We have had a lot of good ones, brother. I am so glad to have you here with us." He pauses and then says, "I probably should not say this, but I always thought we would get married around the same time, to sisters."

He gives me an embarrassed smile, "I know she meant a lot to you at one time."

I nod, "She still does. She saved my life.

He smiles, "I know she did and I know she still cares a lot about you. I saw how dark she went when you left her, Jordan. Paige and I watched her go from the carefree girl to this person we did not recognize anymore. She did not eat. She did not sleep. She lost a lot of weight. Then one day she got it in her head that she was leaving town. She was moving off to college across the country. Her parents both cried. And Paige, she was beside herself. Macy wanted a life away from the memories of you. And she did that for herself. She survived. She is the woman she is today not because of anyone but herself. She pulled herself out of her own hell and survived. I just hope you do not make her fall back into the girl she fought so hard to get away from."

Silence falls over us for a minute and Dylan takes a big breath, letting it out slowly, "I love you, man. You are the brother I always wanted. But if I had to choose, I would choose her. She is my sister now but even without the wedding, she always has been a little sister to me. Paige was so worried about her back then, she almost broke up with me because she felt like she was doing Mace a disservice not being by her side twenty-four -seven. I know what you did was all to protect her but damn man, she deserved to know why."

My eyes flash red at Dylan, "She can never know why. That's part of keeping her safe. She can never know why I did it. After this weekend, please keep her safe. That's all I ask. Take care of her, please."

The chatter continues throughout the car as we get closer to our destination, but Dylan and I sit in mutual silence, understanding each other, even when no words are spoken.

Chapter Sixteen
Macy

After a thirty-minute drive, we enter the town of Aspen, Colorado. It's one of my families favorite places to go when I was younger for luncheons or shopping days. The shops, the eating, it was always so luxurious. We used to come a few times during the winter and snowboard; sometimes Dylan and Jordan got to tag along too.

Turning onto a side road, Mary drives her car to a parking lot in the middle of no where. The girls pile out of the SUV first leaving the men to bring up the rear. Once the last one shuts the door of her suburban, Mary locks her car with a beep, and we all follow her to a big castle building. It's not until we are out of the parking lot and on the front steps of the castle that I realize just how high up in elevation we are.

The building is massive in size, with rock exterior that looks decades old. The snow is still on the ground in this part of elevation and is giving the place a beautiful Christmas card picture background. A poster sign hangs near the front entrance that says, **BEST ESCAPE ROOM OF COLORADO.** Written in smaller letters on the poster it says, **HELP US SAVE SANTA.**

Mary reaches out to open the front iron doors but they are locked. A security camera moves over to us, and after a moment, someone speaks, "Welcome. We have been expecting you. To enter, you must read the sign that is about to pop up on this screen," out of no where a projector screen covers the front doors, "and figure out the riddle. It is the key to learning how to enter our castle. Just a little practice for what is to come. Inside, you will follow the signs to our main desk where Barb will assist you further." The riddle pops up on the screen, "I hope you can help us save Santa!"

The camera moves back to its original angle and we all move closer getting a better view of the riddle.

"Paige reads it aloud, "Looking for a way inside I see, try checking out door #3."

We all look around, but stand confused.

"There are only 2 doors here." Dylan states.

Everyone spreads out, walking along the side of the castle to make sure we are not missing something.

Jordan and I stand at the front door, re reading the riddle over and over.

"Check out door #3." Jordan mumbles again.

"Wait a minute…" I whisper and move closer to the door. The door is large and standing far away, it looks like its just one big door, but there is two handles which means there has to be two doors. I run my hands along the handles, and the length of the doors to the bottom. "Which means maybe there's one hidden…" my hand snags on something that my eyes could not see on their own from far away. A small ring is attached to the bottom of the right door, and I pull it, "Would you look at that." I smirk.

Another door opens within the rocks themselves beside the iron doors. Everyone runs back to the front doors gasping, "How on earth did you figure that out?" Paige squeals.

"Normally these things are right in front of you." I grin.

"Macy is on my team!" Greg jokes and everyone laughs, besides Jordan.

"No one is on teams, dip shit. We are all doing this together." Jordan stares with a clip tone.

I smile, "So possessive." I whisper to him as everyone else walks past us inside the castle.

He leans into my ear, "you damn right."

Entering through the door, it's nothing but a black hallway with Christmas lights draped on the wall. Soft Christmas music pays in the background and we all walk closely together down the hall. Eventually, it opens up into a grand room with chairs, a couch, and a front desk. Jordan walks up beside me as we enter the main lobby with everyone else. The place is dark, lit up with red and green lights and some strobe lights. A woman, standing in an elf costume has a creepy smile on her face while we all stand before her.

"Good morning, Folks." The evil elf says, "My name is Barb. I am one of Santas helpers." She steps forward towards Dylan and Paige, "I'm assuming you two are the bride and groom." They both look at each other shocked that she knew that and nod. "Excellent," she says darkly, "team building is very smart before a wedding, making sure everything goes to plan." She sighs, "I would know. Working in Santa's workshop, you have to be able to all get along or nothing stays on schedule." She turns her back on us and then turns quickly again to face us, "that is why I am here. Santa is no where to be found. Some of the elves have gone mad," she gives an evil chuckle, "and the North Pole is not what it used to be." She hits a red button that is on the desk and a buzzer goes off for a second making us all jump, "we need you to figure out who has done this and find Santa!"

She retreats behind a black curtain when a few evil laughing elves come out from behind a closed door.

"Let's get you to your room." One says in a hoarse voice.

I feel a hand grab my arm. Everyone else follows the elves into the room.

"Jordan,". I giggle, "they are acting."

"Elves?" He whispers, "Why the hell would anyone want to make something so small and cute into evil beings?"

I laugh following the others into the room with him right behind me, "you will survive."

"I may not. Might as well give me one last kiss on my farewell. This is the end. I just know it." He states to me comically.

"If this is the end, I wish you peace." I grin, walking away from him to take a seat with everyone else. He grabs his chest in defeat and takes a seat beside me. The elves leave the room, shutting the door behind them without saying a single word. The only light is the few lamps spaced out around the room. We cannot hear the Christmas music that was playing out in the main area anymore; instead, there is evil laughter and screaming happening every few minutes.

"This isn't creepy or anything." Paige says leaning into me.

"Wait. Where did Mary go?" Dylan asks.

We all look around, but the only ones of us that are in here are the wedding party.

"Maybe one of them kidnapped her." Jordan says leaning back into his seat. "Shit. Should have grabbed her keys before so we could drive away." I giggle, swatting at him, "That is not funny." But the men all seem to think so.

The door opens slowly, a black cloaked figure appears wearing an elf hat and a creepy smile on its face like Barb had.

"I hear you all are here to help us." She circles the couches, stopping behind Frank and Greg, "Well, good luck, or shall I say, break a leg. I mean that legitimately. Because finding the culprit is not what you will achieve. You are too weak. You won't last an hour solving the puzzle."

Another elf comes bouncing in, full of energy, "Kyla! Stop scaring our guests!" The new elf says to creepy Kyla who rolls her eyes at the energetic, but seemingly nice one.

"Sorry for my rude friend. My name is Pinky!" She smiles, "And I am so happy you have decided to help us. Working together is important and is the key to success! I will be leading you to your first room. You have three rooms to enter before the end. You have an hour and half to finish them all. If you are still inside one of them when time runs out, you lose and the evil one will rule the North Pole and all of us."

A creepy smile comes across Kyla's face, "and all of you get to go down with us." A chuckle comes from both of them as a part of the black wall opens.

Jordan leans into me, "Like I was saying, why make elves creepy. This just ruined my thoughts of them."

"You will be the first one they will make an elf." I whisper back to him. His eyes widen, "Um, I thought they were kidding."

Chapter Seventeen
Jordan

Normally, when you are a part of the wedding party, and get invited for a weeklong stay prior to the wedding day, your first thought is- as a man – I am going to be getting laid, a lot. Not sitting in a room full of the wedding party, trying to figure out codes, or some shit, to escape the room we voluntarily agreed to be locked in. I say the word, voluntarily, loosely because technically I am here against my own free will. If I was the one in charge, I would be stealing Mary's car and going elsewhere. Preferably, to a bar or back to the chalet with Macy in my bed.

This place is just absurd, and the elves are creepy as fuck. Creepy tiny Elves that made your hair stand up on your arms and feel like you are in some haunted house. The North Pole is supposed to be cute and magical, not sinister.

"Jordan come help us." Macy orders me.

Paige, Dylan, and Macy are all huddled around a wooden desk in the back of the room, while everyone else is walking around looking at the mysterious art on the wall.

"This must be Santa's office." Dylan says.

"What makes you think that?" Paige asks.

"It could be anyone's office." Macy says, looking through papers.

"I agree with Dylan," I state, resting up against the desk, watching Macy rummage though papers.

She huffs, not looking up but says, "We do not know that for sure."

"I believe I do." I smirk, holding up the plaque that says, **Santa Clause's Desk** so everyone could see it. I was not trying t o be a smart ass but hey, it was an easy find.

Dylan laughs, "Smart ass."

"Proud of yourself, huh?" Macy grins.

"Actually," I start, putting the plaque down, "I'll be happier when we get the hell out of here."

"I think I've found something!" Macy squeals and places a piece of paper in the middle of the desk. Everyone gathers around us, eyeing the paper.

Someone is wanting to take over the North Pole. I have had my suspicions for awhile and I believe it is one of my own elves. If something were to happen to me, please remember my fireplace. The code is right candy cane, left candy cane, forward, and backwards. It will lead the way to Smirf.

Please help me keep the Elves safe.
-SC

"Hmm," Paige starts, "Who could SC be?"

We all stare at her, dumbfounded for a few seconds.

"You cannot be serious." Macy says.

"Think really hard, sweetheart." Dylan says with a smile, reassuring her.

"Well, could it be Scott something?" She asks us.

I chuckle, "Good guest wise one, but let's go with Santa Claus."

We all break out into laughter while Macy rolls her eyes and walks over to the fireplace. It is made of red brick with empty candle holders placed along the top. A fake fire burns inside and a big antique mirror hangs above it.

Macy runs her hands along the tops of it, around the sides, and over the candle holders.

"What are you thinking, Mace?" I ask.

"The note said candy canes, but I don't think there are any." She pauses and runs her hands over the candle holders again. Her hand wobbles on top of the one on the far left and it moves, falling over. We all gasp as a candy cane pops up beside the candle that fell over. Macy goes through the other three candle holders and each time, a candy cane pops up beside it.

"What did that paper say?" She asks us and Dylan grabs the paper again.

"Right, Left, Forward, and Backwards." He reads off the paper.

Macy, Paige, Frank, and I all turn a candy cane where the paper instructed us.

A loud, pop sounds within the fireplace and we all jump back, watching in amazement as the mantle opened up and a secret doorway appears.

"I'm guessing this leads us to room #2?" Macy questions out loud.

"Who is going first?" Paige asks and we all look around at each other.

Macy gives me a reassuring smile and gestures for me to walk on through the new doorway, but I shake my head no and say, "Nope. Not happening. I will gladly wait out the time in here if I have to."

"And be stuck in here with me?" A creepy voice pops up beside me and I scream at the same time.

"Kyla. How long have you been beside me?" I ask, holding my chest.

"I never left." The creepy elf says with an evil grin.

"You know what, I'll take my chances in that new room." I tell everyone as I lead us into the fireplace.

"You are so brave." Macys sarcastic voice rings in my ear as we enter a new room that looks like Santa's workshop.

"Brave is not the word I would use." I pause, "Honestly, I think I almost shit my pants because of that damn elf."

Macy and the other girls chuckle behind me while everyone else finally enter the doorway with us.

A TV high on the wall turns on, with an image of Santa tied to a chair and duct tape over his mouth. A intriguing loud but creepy voice starts to speak, "Smart group. A lot smarter than I gave you credit for. But this room will be much harder. You are in Santa's workshop and somewhere in here is the answer you need to go on to the final room. Unless you want all the kids in the world to see their beloved Santa be no more, you better get to work. Remember, everything you need to know is closer than you think."

The screen goes black and a thirty-minute timer comes on the screen.

"Well, let's get to work gang!" Rylee says to all of us.

Macy laughs, "Okay, Velma."

Walking around the room, some of us going different directions looking over the walls, tables, toys that were being built, and papers.

"What are you thinking detective?" I ask Macy, sliding in behind her at the back table, away from everyone else, as I lean down in her ear.

She smiles, making eye contact with me for a brief moment, and then she does something I was not expecting; Her ass rubs up against my cock.

I'm hard instantly.

INSTANTLY

"You need to stop before I take you right here in front of everyone." I growl into her ear.

Everyone is oblivious as they search the room; I could care less about escaping this damn building now.

"Oh, I don't know what you are talking about." Macy grins at me.

Her ass moving back and forth slower this time as she bends down farther into me acting like she's looking for something on the ground.

I grab her waist, making her stand back up, and step closer, pinning her in between the table and me, lowering my lips to her ear, I nibble. A slow breath leaves her, and I tell her, "Do that again, Mace, and I don't care who sees me rip your pants apart right here while I have an appetizer."

I back away slowly, removing my arm from her waist as she whimpers.

"I think I found something!" Dylan says across the room and everyone else runs over to see what he found.

I grab a paper from the table Macy and I were at and place it in front of my jeans to cover my hard cock until it goes away, but as I look back at Macy, her mouth open in an O and her cheeks blushing, I don't know if it will go away.

Chapter Eighteen
Macy

Flustered is not the word I would call my emotions right now. The North Pole can be taken over for all I care, the throb in between my legs needs to be taken care of. Call me selfish – I really do not give a shit. I may regret this later but right now I choose to be the naughty girl who needs her release right now. Put me on the naughty list Santa. This man and his gorgeous body, his eyes, and the way he speaks to me... I know I am just asking for trouble.

Walking up to Jordan, who stands in the back of everyone listening to what Dylan found, I Wrap my arm around his forearm. I pull him back with me and whisper, "Want to be put on Santa's naughty list with me?"

His eyes twinkle at me and a smirk spreads over his face, "You read my damn mind."

While everyone else is occupied, he leads me back to the first room through the fireplace.

"Do you think Red, or Yellow, or whatever her name was will be here? Or the creepy one?" I ask, holding his hand as we enter the room.

"If they are, they are about to get a fucking show." Jordan says while pushing me up against the wall as soon as we enter the first room. His chest presses into me and his lips crash down onto mine. I grip a handful of his hair in between my fingers and pull them lightly as he moves to my neck.

"Jordan." I moan slowly, "We are going to get caught."

He pulls off my neck. Methodically, he runs his thumb over my lip, and slowly, he guides his hand down my torso and lifts my leg to hang around him. He smiles, "I sure hope so."

We turn erotic, both of my legs wrap around him as he sits me down on the desk, leaning me down slowly so my back is on the top.

"Told you I wanted an appetizer." He smirks, unwrapping my legs and pushing them apart. Slowly unbuttoning my jeans, I lift my hips as he guides them down my thighs.

He leans down, running his tongue carefully over my panties which makes me moan from the stimulation alone.

"Why are you smiling?" I ask him curiously.

"I've missed the taste of you." He smiles sliding my panties down exposing me.

"You always were ready for me." He says, eyeing the wetness in my panties.

"Well chow down big boy." I joke.

He doesn't give me time to react as he devours me like his last meal. Sucking, licking, penetrating with his tongue, he does it all while I buck my hips under him. Clasping my thighs around his head as he sucks over my already sensitive clit, a moan escapes from my lips.

"That a girl. Clamp those thighs, take all the oxygen away from me." He sucks even harder, "You always were a good girl."

His words almost tip me over the edge, "Oh My God." I moan.

"Come on Macy, cum all over my face." He tells me, "I think I know what you need," He inserts a finger into me and my eyes roll back. A second finger enters and the bastard looks up with a cocky grin, "Come for me, Mace. Be a good girl and soak me."

Between his words, his fingers pumping in and out, and his mouth sucking over my clit, I feel my toes curl as my orgasm erupts over me. My cries of pleasure, I'm sure, echoing through the entire castle.

"Oh. My. God" We jump at the sound of someone else in the room.

Jumping up and pulling my panties up, Jordan jumps in front of me to cover me, but my face flushes red when I notice we aren't alone.

The entire wedding party is staring at us, wide eyed and mouths wide open.

My sister's eyes are looking back and forth at us in shock but Dylan looks like he wants to kill Jordan, and I think I might die of embarrassment because I just looked up and saw a fucking camera is in this room.

"Um, we can explain." Jordan says.

"Jordan. Fucking. Smith." Dylan erupts as his right fist hits Jordan so hard it knocks him out.

"What the fuck, Dylan!" Paige and I both say in unison.

Chapter Nineteen
Jordan

My eyes flutter open, and suddenly I am reaching for my head as a headache takes over. I jump up but a hand goes to my chest.

Mace.

"What happened?" I groan, laying back on the pillows. I'm in our bedroom in the chalet.

She gives me a soft smile, grabbing a water by the nightstand and handing it to me.

"Well, Dylan knocked your ass out." She laughs.

"I meant with the escape room. Did we win? Did we save Santa?" I joke

Macy laughs again. That laugh I could listen to over and over again. She says, "No, not after you fell out cold. They all were coming back into room one because they could hear something loud happening in there." She looks embarrassed, "and they saw us. Mary was waiting for us in the lobby, but apparently there's cameras in every room and they told her that we all had to leave because one of the couples were having sex in one of the rooms."

I let out a big horse laugh.

"So Mary came in right after Dylan knocked you out. Me and you are being fined $500 for PDA and for them to pay a cleaning crew to clean the room we were in." She giggles, "You will be paying it by the way, since it is your fault." But she then goes serious, "And Dylan wanted you in a car home. But I talked him out of it. He's the only one who is really mad. Even my parents had suspected it and you know Paige always wanted us to get married one day and have babies." She mocks.

I almost spit my water everywhere.

"I need to go talk to Dylan" I tell her, sitting the water back down.

"I agree. He is in the gym in the basement." She advises me before standing up and heading to the bedroom door.

"Mace?" I question her, and when she looks at me I state, "I meant what I said earlier, that was just an appetizer. I'll have my main course when I return."

She smiles, her cheeks turning pink, "What a disservice if I let you starve."

***

Dylan is throwing punches at the punching bag when I enter the gym. He's shirtless, only wearing gym shoes and basketball shorts and sweat is beading down his body.

"Imagining it's me?" I ask, startling him as I get closer.

"Yep." He replies in a clipped tone, throwing a few more punches.

"Well, here I am now, brother. Use me instead of that poor bag." I tell him.

He gives a couple more hard punches and a couple jabs, "Not unless I want to kill you, and we both know I do not really want that."

"Oh come on man. You had to have an idea." I know I'm playing with fire but he is my best friend. The only one besides Macy who knows the life I came from.

He turns quickly, the pulse in his neck pumping hard, "I told you she was off limits, Smith."

I put my hands up in surrender, "Then why did your fiancé try so hard to get us to get along. The bear incident? What the hell was all of that?" I ask him.

"Get along, yes. Not fuck her in the middle of an escape room." He yells at me. "We both know you and her have a past. We both know what will happen if you both become a thing again." He gets nose to nose with me, "Would you really be so selfish that you would put her in harms way again?"

My nostrils flare, "Don't you dare question me like that."

Dylan turns around, holding his arms out wide and starts punching the bag again, "Seems to me like you want her hurt. You want her harmed. All so you can get your selfish fix of her."

I grab his shoulders, pulling him back so hard from the bag he lands on the ground, "As I recall, I almost got myself killed because of wanting to keep her safe."

He jumps up, eyeing me and shakes his head, "I don't like this, Smith. You are playing with fire."

"Don't you think I know that?" I yell, "She was my best friend, Dylan. Other than you, she was my person. She was the person I wanted to live the rest of my life with. She took my heart that night on the ridge and she has had it sense." A tear wells in my eyes, "I would die before something happened to her."

Dylan's hand lightly touches my shoulder, "You and me both brother."

"Then let's do what we promised we would do years ago. Protect her." We both nod in agreement. I add, "But this weekend, she will be with me. And nothing you say will change that."

He smirks, but surrenders.

Chapter Twenty
Jordan 17 years old

All the guys rush out of the football locker room going separate ways after practice, leaving Dylan and I to be the only ones left. Pulling my shirt over my head after drying off from the shower, Dylan sits down by my gym bag waiting on me.

"I figured you'd need a ride home. The girls want us to meet them at the ice cream place before we go." He states.

I nod, "Thanks, man." I toss my towel through my wavy hair one last time before throwing it in to the dirty towel hamper.

We both grab our gym bags and head out of the gym, turning the lights off and locking the door behind us. Dylan's phone rings, "Hey ba-...Whoa, Paige, wait a minute. Slow down baby, what is wrong?" He turns to me, panic written all over his face. "Stay where you are. Jordan is with me. We are coming. Hang on." I hear Paige screaming on the other end, but no actual sentences are making sense, "Baby, take deep breaths, please breathe. I'm coming."

He runs towards his car, and I follow. Jumping inside, he throws it in reverse and gravel flies all behind us as we leave the school parking lot.

"Dylan, what's going on?" I'm starting to worry now.

His white nuckles grip his steering wheel, "It's Macy."

His words go out as black enters my mind. All the what ifs making my adrenaline run wild. My heart is pumping fast through my veins I think I could fly to get to her right now if I had to. I blink and we are pulling up at Paige and Macy's favorite ice cream shop, Paige is pacing out the front.

The car doesn't stop good yet before I am barreling out and grabbing Paige by the shoulders, "Paige. Where is Mace?" I yell. Tears flow down her face as she points to their car and I run. Flinging the door open, Macy sits in the front seat, holding her head, shaking and crying.

"Hey. Baby. Look at me. It's Jordan." Her eyes snap up to me and she claws at me holding on for life. I notice her eye looks bruised, with a cut over the top, and her shirt is torn.

Trying to steady my breathing, I hold her as close as I can, "Shhh, baby. It's okay. It's okay. Tell me what happened."

***

Macy
Present Day

It is rehearsal dinner and the bridesmaid's luncheon today. The groomsmen are going out for their own luncheon while us girls go do our own things and we all will meet back up at the wedding venue for rehearsal this evening. The sun is coming through the windows of the kitchen while I fix a glass of orange juice. Turning to put the orange juice back in the fridge, I jump when my father enters the room. He is still in his sleep clothes; a pants and top pj set my mom usually buys them to match.

"Good morning, sweetheart." He says, kissing me on the cheek.

"Hey, daddy." I smile.

He takes a coffee cup from the cabinet and pours him some coffee, by the vacant noise throughout the house, it seems everyone else is still upstairs in their rooms.

He places the coffee pot back in the maker and takes a sip of his cup, leaning back into the counter.

"Do you want to talk about it?" I ask him, embarrassed.

"I'm not stupid, Mace." He smirks, "I knew about you and Jordan when you two were kids. Even though I played dumb, I kept an eye on him more than you think." He winks.

I nod, "I know daddy. Thank you for helping him."

"I went to high school with his father. He was always a rough guy. He did not come from a good home life either. The apple does not fall far from the tree usually," He pauses, "but I am happy to say Jordan was one of the lucky ones."

I smile, "Because of you and Dylan's dad."

He gives a soft smile and says, "No, we just helped pave the way for him. We showed him what could happen with hard work and people cheering

128

for you and caring about you. He needed that push. He knew he wanted a better life; we just helped him see it was possible."

"Well, I never told him that you helped pay for his college tuition or any of that." I grin.

"You kept our little secret?" His eyebrow lifted.

"You told me to, didn't you?" I smile.

"Yes, because I did not want him knowing who gave him a second chance. I wanted him to think he did it all himself. I wanted him to know how strong he really was." He takes a sip of his drink. "I just didn't think my daughter would fall in love with him." He smiles.

My cheeks blush, "That was a long time ago. This thing now, I don't know what it is, but I am thankful for the time my heart got back of him at least for the week."

He nods, "Macy, you two were always meant to be together. He loved you and by the way he looks at you now, he still does"

I stay silent, unsure what to say next so I eventually change the subject

"Daddy, thank you for all the money you put into his education, and making sure he was going to make it. The money you gave his mother so they could keep their house, the good words you put into coaches so he got a scholarship. You will never know how thankful I am for you. I wish everyone got to have a father like you." I sit down my orange juice and hug him.

My father takes a deep breath while he hugs me back, "You and your sister are my world, princess. Jordan saved your life." I pull back just in time to see his nostrils flare, "That night he brought you home with that bruise on your eye and your clothes torn, I saw red. Macy, I almost committed murder that night."

My eye glistens with a tear, "I think you, Jordan, and Dylan all three almost did." I giggle, "So are you sure you are okay with all of this?"

"Honestly, no. But if I had to approve anyone for you, it would be Jordan Smith. I know he will protect you, no matter what." He kisses my cheek, sitting his coffee cup in the sink, "Okay, enough sappy talk. I need to go bother your mother." He winks at me and I make a disgusted face, knowing what that meant.

Chapter Twenty – One
Paige

"I cannot believe she didn't tell me." I fall back on the bed in my bedroom while Dylan pulls his pants up and throws his shirt back on. "She is my best friend. Why would she keep this from me?"

Dylan walks over and kisses me softly on the lips, "Jordan kept it from me too, babe. Maybe they were afraid it would ruin our weekend."

I smile, his baggy tshirt hanging over my thighs as I sit up, "I cannot wait to be your wife."

He nods, "I have been dreaming of this day for a long time."

He can tell something is on my mind so he eyes me curiously, I shrug, "I just always thought Macy and I would marry brothers." She winks, "I always thought her And Jordan would get married. Why did he do it?"

Dylan huffs, "You know I cannot tell you."

I pout, "Right. You are sworn to such a secret that even your own wife cannot know about it."

He grins, "It's because I do not want you in the middle of it. If I told you, it would put you in harms way."

I cock an eyebrow, "And Macy? Is she in harms way?" She huffs, "Dylan I swear if there is something you are not telling me that I need to know about my sister I will call this wedding off."

His hand goes to my shoulder and he stares at me for a long moment, "Sweetheart, I promise. Jordan has assured me she will not be in danger. Neither will you."

"Good." I cross my arms, "I finally got her back in the same space as me, Dill. I don't want to lose her again."

He nods, agreeing but stays silent.

After a moment of more kissing, Dylan leaves me in the room to get ready for the day but as I get to the bathroom and look in the mirror a memory takes over...

Paige
17 years old

"Get in loser, we are going to get ice cream." I scream at my sister who is getting out of cheerleading practice.

"You buying?" She grins at me.

I wave our fathers credit card up in the air, the one he gave us for emergencies only. By the way my stomach is growling right now, I'd say it's a pretty big emergency. Macy

132

smiles, drops her gym bag in the backseat, and plops down in the passenger seat beside me.

"Dylan is driving Jordan home after practice, so I texted him and told him to meet up at the creamery downtown." I tell Macy while pulling out of the school parking lot and heading out on the main road.

We talk about our school day and how Macy's cheer practice went up until we pull up at the creamery. It's the place Macy and I have loved since we were children. Decorated on the outside like a cabin, but on the inside, it is lined with booths, both big and small, and tables throughout the middle of the room with chairs. A long counter with a glass dome cover is where all the ice cream is kept so you can pick your flavors and toppings. Our parents brought us here as kids and now that we have boyfriends, it is our favorite hang out.

I pull into the parking lot, noticing the neon open sign as I pull in. Getting out, it does not look to be too busy as we head inside.

"Hey girls!" Heather, the owner and a good friend of our parents, says as we step inside and head up to the counter, "The usual I presume?" She smiles and we nod.

"Are the boys coming too?" She asks us as she scoops up our ice cream.

"Yeah, the usual for them too, please." Macy answers her while I pay the cashier for our order.

We grab all four ice creams and find an empty booth to sit in.

Music plays softly in the background and without saying a word, both of us dive into our ice cream not waiting on the boys.

The front door dings, but neither of us pay attention to who comes through the door until we hear Heather say, "You know I won't serve you. Get out."

Macy and I turn to see who she is talking to, and I turn to Macy in horror, "Macy, hide."

"I said, GET OUT!" Heather screams but the man she's yelling at turns to pick up a chair and throws it across the counter at her. Her and her staff duck just in time so it misses them.

Macy tries to get up out of the booth, but as soon as she stands up, the man's eyes lock on her.

Heather looks at Macy and I and screams, "Girls. RUN."

We get out of the booth and take off running, I get out the door but realize quickly that Macy is not with me. "Macy!" I scream, turning around to see the man picking her up and tossing her across the creamery.

"No!" I yell running back inside. "Leave her alone!"

The man hits my sister, over and over while crawling on top of her and pulling at her clothes. I jump on his back, kicking and screaming but my weight is nothing for him and he tosses me to the ground beside Macy.

Heather comes out from behind the counter, holding a gun in his face, "Get off the girls." She says coldly to him. And the most evil grin crosses his face, "Or what?" He says in a very testing manner.

She cocks the gun, putting her finger on the trigger, "Or I shoot." She states.

His smile leaves and he stands up slowly, holding his hands up in surrender, eyeing me and Macy, "I'm not done here." He tells us, "You better tell my so-called son he has not seen the last of me. Trying to make this better life for himself just won't do."

The not so Best Man

The man turns and walks out of the front door, and as soon as he is out of sight, I fall to my knees, grabbing Macy in my arms and holding on to her for life as tears run down her face.

Her cries fill the building and I know now the severity of the situation we are in. I thought Dylan was being dramatic when he told me weeks ago this man was dangerous.

Twenty- Two
Macy

The ladies are all out to a luncheon before the rehearsal dinner tonight. My mother rented out a beautiful Italian restaurant for us to dine at while my father and the men all went to a sports bar to have some guy time. We arrive and all park outside the beautiful rock building, laced with a variety of landscaping plants and trees along the front.

"This place is beautiful, mom." I tell my mother once we head inside, and I sit down beside her. Paige sits on the other side of her while the rest of the bridesmaids fill up the remaining seats of the long table they sat us at.

"I know how much my girls love Italian food." She grins.

A tear pricks her eye, "You two are my greatest blessing in this life. I hope you know how proud I am of you." She turns to me, "How proud I am of the women you both are."

A tear makes my eyes twinkle, "Thanks, mommy."

The waiter comes up to us, a tall Italian man who looks like he should be the head of a mafia gang.

He smiles at us all then says, "Evening ladies, I hope you are having a wonderful day." He looks between all of us, "I hear there is a bride in our midst, let me see if I can guess who it is." He walks around our table, carefully taking us all in, but suddenly stops when he gets to Paige, and says, "I think we have a winner gentlemen."

The lights go low and music that sounds like it comes from Magic Mike starts playing. Shirtless waiters all come out from behind the door that I thought led to the kitchen. My mouth hangs open and I look at my mother, "You did not."

She smirks, "Strippers are a must for a wedding week."

I lay my head back in a horse laugh as Paige's eyes go wide, "Mother!" She squeals and the waiters pick her chair up with her in it and bring it to the stage that I just assumed was for karaoke.

Nope, it's for the strippers who are about to invade my sister.

The men all circle her, and some take off their suspenders and let them hang by their legs and Paige covers her eyes. My mother is eating it up as she hoots and hollers. The other bridesmaids follow suit, but I cannot help and just giggle the entire time.

"I think this one wants to be blindfolded men." Our waiter says, since Paige covered her eyes.

They grab her hands away from her eyes and place a black silky blindfold over them. The waiter looks at all of us and says, "I think she has been a naughty girl."

Paige squeals, "No. I'm a good girl. I promise."

I laugh, "Mom, she is never going to forgive you."

Mom leans into me and says, "Poor me. What will I ever do."

I grin, "What are the men doing? Are they really at a bar?"

Mom smirks and that tells me all I need to know.

Jordan

"Brian, what did you do?" I ask, looking around at the strippers all around us.

"It was Kristina's idea, not mine. I just went along with it." He smiles.

"I hope one day I am a cool parent like you." My eyes widen as soon as the words leave my mouth. I have not thought about having children in a long time. Not since Macy and I broke up. I always thought she would be my wife one day, carry my children, grow old with me. But that was then, and this is now. Just because we have been sleeping together doesn't mean it can go any farther, whether I wanted it to or not. It just won't ever be possible if I want to keep her safe.

Brian chuckles, "You will be. Those little girls were the best thing to ever happen to me. Then you and Dylan came along and you boys were the sons I never got to have biologically. Thank you for being in our life."

I smile, taking a sip of my beer, "Thank you, sir. For all you did."

He nods but stays silent, turning to the stage where Dylan is sitting in a chair blindfolded. I got pay back earlier from him hitting me in the escape room. We were wrestling in the car on the way here and I grabbed him around the neck, cutting off air until he was out snoozing. Brian had told me earlier a just of what we were doing today, and while I don't necessarily want it done to me, I was all for getting this fucker back for the bear incident.

"He is going to be so pissed." I lean into the table so Brian could hear me as the music starts playing.

Brain laughs, "Don't worry, I called in a favor with the wedding planner.

My eyes widen, "The Wedding Planner?"

Brian smirks as Dylan wakes up and they remove his blindfold.

"You assholes!!" He yells and we all giggle.

The strippers go off stage and the spotlight hits Dylan while he yells, "Paige will break off the wedding over this. Get me down."

Brian winks at me and then turns to Dylan, "I know my daughter, and I have something planned where she will never look at you the same."

Dylan's eyes widen, "Brian, please don't. She will be so mad." He moves his eyes to me, "Jordan, please talk some sense into him. Paige is not forgiving."

I laugh, "This is for the bear incident and you knocking me out at the escape room, fucker."

"Oh come on now." Dylan squeals trying to break out of his chair restraints.

"We are ready for you" Brian yells to someone I cannot see. The stage curtains move, and I about spit my beer all over the place when I see who comes out from behind it.

"Miss me, Sugar?" Pinky and Kyla, the creepy elves from the escape room, say to Dylan as they get into his line of view.

He screams, like full on murderous screams. "You fuckers!! Get these creeps away from me!"

"Come on, you don't want to play?" Kyla says, dark and low, with a grin that looks sinister.

Pinky laughs, "We brought friends."

I'm horrified when I see Barb and all the other elves from the escape room, creepy as hell, walking onto the stage slowly and making their way to Dylan. Some are holding big candy canes, one is scratching its nails across the stage slowly, and they all surround Dylan. He jerks, trying to get out of the hold the chair has him in, and when Kyla gets in his

140

face again, he screams so loud I thought my glass beer would break.

Brian doubles over laughing and waves at the person in the dark side of the room, "Okay, bring your camera out."

The wedding photographer who Mary had hired comes out with her assistant while still taking photos of Pinky and Kyla terrorizing Dylan as he screams. I slap Brian on the back, "Remind me never to piss you off if this is what you are capable of."

He smiles, "Hurt my daughter again and you will find out." He pats me on the back.

I smile, but as soon as he turns away, my smile fades. They will all hate me after this weekend.

Chapter Twenty- Three
Macy

My breath hitches as I take a step inside the wedding venue tonight before the rehearsal dinner. The beautiful venue sits on acres of land, surrounded by woods, and the building is an identical rendition of The Biltmore Estate in North Carolina. We went there once on a family vacation when Paige and I were kids. She said she wanted to get married there one day but then they built this wedding venue in Aspen, and she swore it was fate telling her she HAD to get married here.

Mary has gone above and beyond for this night. The long aisles with pews on each side are draped with white roses and a beautiful arch is at the end. Low, instrumental music plays quietly in the background while each of us enter the chapel.

"Mary!" Paige squeals, "It is everything I sent you on my Pinterest board."

I laugh, "Why am I not shocked you sent her your Pinterest."

My dad's voice rings behind us, "You better love it for what I'm paying for it."

We all giggle and Paige hugs our father tight.

Pulling out of their hug, Paige looks at me, "You have one too! Don't even come at me over it." She turns back to Mary and hugs her.

I feel someone come up close behind me, his warm breath on my ear as he says, "A wedding Pinterest board? I need to see that."

I shriek, "I cannot show you."

Jordan's arm rests on my hip and he asks, "Why not."

I pull out my phone from my clutch and show him.

A small smile creases his lips as he whispers the name of my board, "**Jordan and Macy's happily ever after.**"

My cheeks flush from embarrassment, "It was a long time ago so don't read too much into it."

"When did you make that?" He asks, hoarsely this time.

I shrug grinning, "I think it was after the night you ate my terrible cooking."

When my eyes meet his, I can tell he is off in a deep thought; I know the exact one he is seeing right now.

Jordan
17 years old

"You sure you know how to cook?" I ask Macy while she pulls the brownies from the oven.

A few minutes before she took them out, the smoke detector went off, alerting us that something was smoking. In her defense, I was distracting her a little bit.

Her parents are gone this weekend and Paige is staying over at Dylan's, yet again. So, Macy and I have the entire house to ourselves. Thankfully, we ordered pizza to eat, but she insisted she could cook us brownies for dessert. I knew she was full of shit but her little pout when she thought I was going to decline her offer made me agree to let her cook for me, against my better judgment, of course.

The smile on her face was worth every bit of agony I will have eating these poor brownies and lying to her when I tell her they taste good.

"Here." she says, sitting the plate with a piece of the fresh brownie on it in front of me while giving me a fork to take a bite. Smiling at me like her life depends on it, I know she won't leave until she watches me take a bite. Honestly, I wish she would turn around so I could throw it down the sink, but she knows me too well.

I don't let my grin waiver as I take the fork from her and stick it into the warm brownie. Pulling the fork up to my mouth, I put all of it in and smile, nodding my head in acceptance.

"So, it's good? You approve?" She asks all giddy.

I give her a thumbs up as I swallow the dreadful shit that is in my mouth, then I ask, "What did you put in them?"

She waves me off, turning around to get her a piece from the stove, "Oh, just some cocoa, milk, eggs, butter, and I thought it needed a little bit of something new so I put some pickles."

Hmm, odd since I tasted something more...fishy. "Is that all?" I ask.

"Well, I experimented with some sushi mom had leftover in the fridge from the other night's dinner." She says nonchalantly.

My stomach gurgles, "Raw fish?"

"Mhm." She says, taking a bite.

Her face turns three shades of green as the bite hits her mouth. She slowly swallows and looks at me, "You ass! That does not taste good."

I laugh, "Well, I was trying to be nice, but please never cook again. Don't experiment or you'll end up killing someone."

She swats at me and giggles, "Jerk."

I take a deep breath and grab her arm, pulling her into me. Looking into her eyes, I brush her hair out from her eye and place it behind her ear. I grin, "I love you. I have loved you since the moment you saved my life. I want to marry you someday."

Her hands cup my face, and she kisses me softly. "I love you too." She turns walking back to the stove and says, "When I become your wife someday, just remember, lie to me again about my cooking and it'll be a bad day for you." She grins.

I smile, "I promise to never lie to you unless it's for your own good."

Chapter Twenty- Four
Jordan

"Jordan?" Mary's voice rings into my ears, popping me out of a memory that feels like another lifetime ago.

"Hmm?" I ask dazed but quickly realizing everyone is staring at me.

"I was saying how it was bad luck for the bride and groom to stand up there for rehearsal." She points to Macy and then back to me, "So why don't you two do the honors and let them watch you."

"Oh," I mumble, "Sure."

"Lovely!" She claps, "Okay, where is your father?" She asks Macy, but spots him before Macy could reply, "Brian!" Mary waves him down, "We will need you for this as well."

"Oh, Goodie." Brian groans with a sarcastic smile.

"Okay, Everyone who is not Dylan and Paige, follow me. Jordan, go stand up there by the arch." Mary directs everyone.

I give Macy one last reassuring smile and head off down the aisle, so I do not get yelled at by the crazy girl scout wedding lady.

At one point in my life, I thought I would be standing in this exact spot, marrying this woman who is about to walk towards me. She was supposed to be end game for me, the one I grew old with, the one I had my children with, and my best friend. But things change, and keeping her safe had to come before what my heart wanted.

"Okay," Mary starts, "I already gave the bridesmaids and groomsmen their instructions. Paige and Dylan, pay attention to what Jordan and Macy do."

"Do not pay attention to me," I joke, "I still do not know what I'm doing."

Macy's laugh rings through my ears and my heart flutters.

Oh to hear her laugh like that everyday.

Mary rolls her eyes at me, "Stop being a smart ass. This is serious." She points at Macy, "When she gets to you, I will instruct you. Just stand there and look handsome."

I cheese at her and salute, "Yes captain."

"The bridesmaids and groomsmen will go first. Once they get to their assigned sides, another song will start. Macy and Brian, walk carefully and slowly down the aisle. You want to think of gliding more than walking. When the second song starts, count to five then begin." Mary instructs. She turns to Paige and Dylan and yells, "Did y'all hear me?"

They both nod as music takes over the surround sound. The bridesmaids and groomsmen start gliding down the aisle. Mary is chatting on and on about something, but all I can hear is my heartbeat fluttering with each anticipated second of seeing Macy again. Frank and Rylee bring up the rear, and as they part ways, I notice Brian and Macy are not there anymore. I look around but I don't see them. The music changes softly and the sweetest melody of violins is heard, and just as Mary instructed, five seconds past the song starting, Macy comes from one side of the entry way meeting her father on the other, locking arms, and starts walking down the aisle towards me.

My heart hammers in my chest, watching the girl of my dreams, the girl who saved my life so many years ago, walk towards me in this beautiful wedding venue. She looks so beautiful and her smile lights up the room but quickly becomes blurry in my eye. I put my finger up to stop the tear from falling and grin back. When they get a few pews from me, I step off the main stage that I am on and stand in front of them.

Mary comes up to us, "Now Jordan, this is where her father gives her to you." She turns to Brian, "The officiant will say his line and you will say…" she pauses to give him time to answer.

"Her mother and I do." Brian says a little choked up.

Mary nods, "and then you will place her hand in his." Mary turns to Paige and Dylan, who's eyes are glued to us, watching our every move. Paige wipes a tear.

Brian takes Macys hand and places it in mine, "Now you two will step up on the stage together" Mary states.

I lead her beside me as we step up on the stage together, turning to face one another, still holding hands.

"You sure you guys haven't done this before?" Mary asks with a laugh, "Because I never instructed you to do that, but it's exactly what I wanted you to do."

My eyes never leave Macy's, but I chuckle, "Nope. Just felt natural."

Macy's thumb runs over mine and she grins.

"Who knows, I may be planning your wedding one day." Mary jokes.

Macy giggles and it feels like knives are hitting my heart. After this weekend, she will hate me. What I would give for this to be real. For tomorrow to be our big day, but that is not possible if I want to keep her safe. If I want to keep her alive.

Her heart won't be the only one breaking this weekend. Mine will shatter too.

I'll be considered the not so best man after tomorrow.

Chapter Twenty-Five
16 years old
Macy

The other girls I cheer with all wave goodbye as they get in their cars to leave practice. My legs sway as I sit on the concrete wall that surrounds the auditorium where our practices are held. Jordan's football practice should be over with soon and this is where we normally meet.

"Hey beautiful." Jordan's voice sounds behind me. I turn around in time to kiss him on the cheek and he grins.

"What sounds good to eat?" He asks me while taking my hand.

"Let's go get some tacos." I smile really big, and he laughs, knowing I love tacos and could eat them everyday.

"I told Dylan we would meet him and Paige at our favorite Ice cream shop afterwards." He states and I nod.

I trip over my feet as we enter the student parking lot, and my bag of books fall to the ground. Jordan helps me up and bends down to pick up my books, his shirt rides up and that's when I notice something.

He is bruised. His entire lower back is almost black.

"Jordan." I gasp, "What happened?"

He shrugs, still picking up my books, and when he stands, he says, "I'm okay, Macy. My mouth just got a little overloaded."

Grabbing his forearm so he will look at me, I wince, "Your dad is back home?"

He nods but stays silent.

"I'm going to kill him." My tone is clipped. "Jordan, he could have paralyzed you. Or worse."

He ignores me, opening my car door, finally he says, "As long as he is hitting me, he is not hitting my mother. It's okay."

"It is NOT okay!" I yell. "Your mother needs to be a mother and take up for you!"

He lowers his head in embarrassment, and I cup his face, "I'm sorry but it's true. She needs to stand up for you. If she won't, I will."

"No!" Anger forces out of Jordan's mouth, "Macy please, whatever you do, do not provoke him. He will hurt you. And if he hurts you, so help me I will rot in a jail cell." He kisses my forehead, "Promise me."

A tear wells in my eye, "I can't promise I won't defend the person I love if they are getting attacked. I'm sorry Jordan, I will not stand by and do nothing. You are not alone."

His forehead steadies on mine, "I know what he is capable of. Provoking him means he won't stop until you are no longer a threat."

I take a deep breath, "You once told me that no one cared about you. You were so upset about it that you almost ended your life. I'll be damned if I let that happen again."

***

Macy
16 Years old

Jordan would be so upset if he knew what I was about to do. He has told me time and time again for me to stay away from his house. He did not feel it was safe for me to be there in case his father showed up. While sitting in class today, he got a text from his mom saying that his dad was home, so he elected to hang out tonight with some guys at the bowling alley and then go home with Dylan. Paige and I are supposed to meet them there tonight and bowl with them. Right about now, he has most likely come to the conclusion that I would not be arriving with Paige. I lied to her and told her I would get a ride with one of the other girls because I had some homework to finish first.

Thankfully, she did not try to push the issue or catch my lie.

I walked the five blocks to the trailer park, my heart rate accelerating with each step.

Each step telling me I need to go back; I need to just leave it alone.

But seeing those bruises on Jordans back a few days ago, it snapped something inside me. He does not deserve any of what his dad does to him. And his mom is a coward for letting it happen. KNOWING it's happening to her son, and she won't intervene.

Coward.

I'll stand up for him. I'll make sure he is never hit again, even if I have to put the bullet in his father myself.

Staring at the trailer, the porch light is on, and some lights on the inside too. I see his mom move around the living room and I take a deep breath, if his father is not home, maybe I can still talk some sense into her.

Slowly taking the steps leading up to the porch, I grab the handle of the screen door and pull it open. The main door is wide open and Jordan's mom turns to face me, her eyes are blood shot.

"Macy. Hello dear." She pulls at her clothes and combs her hands through her hair.

"Hello Mrs. Smith." I smile, "May I come in for a moment?" I ask.

She looks around the room. Worry is all I see on her face but then she says, "How about I come out on the porch with you."

I smile, "Sure."

We take a seat on the plastic chairs sitting on the front porch. Both of us stay quiet for a moment, then she says, "Figured you'd be with Jordan tonight at the bowling alley."

"Yes ma'am. I plan to go there after I leave. I just wanted to come talk to you and his father first." Her eyes shoot up to mine.

"Wh-why do you want to speak to Allen?" She asks, concerned.

"Because I don't take too well to my boyfriend having bruises all over him." I tell her the truth.

She drops her eyes to the floor and then back up at me, "Macy, please don't. You do not understand."

I shake my head, "I understand perfectly, Mrs. Smith. Is his father here?"

She nods, "He is in the shower. You need to leave before he knows you are here."

I look confused, "Why?"

BANG

The screen door slams open, making both of us jump in our seats.

"What's going on out here?" Jordan's father says while walking out on the porch in shorts, a tshirt, and wet hair; obviously just got out of the shower.

Mrs. Smith jumps to her feet, walking over to her husband and introducing me to him, "Honey, this is Macy, Jordan's girlfriend. She came by for a minute but was just leaving." She eyes me hard on the last word.

"Why leave so early?" His evil grin goes to me, "Stay for awhile, I'm sure Jordan will be home soon."

"Actually, Mr. Smith, I came to speak with you if you do not mind taking a seat so we can talk." I tell him.

He is surprised at my confidence, but finally takes a seat, still wearing a smirk of sin.

I notice Mrs. Smith is uncomfortable now by the way she sat down beside her husband.

"I appreciate you both taking the time to hear me out," I start, "I have noticed a few things lately and want to express my concern."

"And what might that be?" Allen smirks.

"Well, Mr. Smith, the bruises you leave on your son do not sit well with me. Now, I have not gone to the law about it yet, but if it keeps happening, I will make sure the whole town knows." I threaten him.

"You little bitch." Allen snarls, "You are terribly mistaken, we love our son. He fell, that's what the bruises are from."

I look at Mrs. Smith, who now holds her tear-filled eyes on the floor.

I look at her while ignoring her husband, "Mrs. Smith, do you know how Jordan and I met?"

She shakes her head no.

"Jordan was about to jump to his death off the big ridge one night when he and I crossed paths. His exact words to me were that no one would care if he was gone." My eyes hold hers.

Her eyes shoot up to mine, and for a moment, I think she is going to cry, but her eyes just go back to the ground.

Allen jumps to his feet and in two steps he is in front of me, grabbing my arm and pulling me to my feet in front of him.

Slap.

His hand slaps my face. Tears well in my eyes. He bends down to my ear and whispers, "You will leave my property right now, and don't you even think about the law. Call them and I'll make sure your family never sees you again."

I look up at him with a grin, "I'm not afraid of you like your wife is. Mess with Jordan again and I will make sure you rot in a jail cell. If it comes it, I'll put the bullet in you myself."

He pushes me down to the ground, I hit with a thud. My vision goes blurry for a moment and what sounds like a car pulls up in the driveway.

"Mace!!" Jordan's voice echoes in my ears.

Dylan and Jordan run up on the porch, "Dylan, grab Macy. Get her out of here."

Dylan grabs me, but I fight at him, "I am not leaving you, Jordan."

"Get in the damn car." Jordan yells at me.

"Let's go." Dylan says.

Allen swings at Jordan but, thankfully, Jordan is not as small as he was when we first met. Football and workouts have allowed him to grow muscles in places he used to be skin and bones. He lays into his dad. Punch after punch. His mom stands, screaming for him to stop.

Dylan and I reach the car and I turn around in time to see Jordan stand, a bloody hand, and say, "Come at her again and I will kill you."

He walks off the porch towards us, and I run into his arms. His hand goes to my head, and he scans me over, "I love you, crazy girl. Please never do that again."

I kiss him. A deep and passionate kiss. Coming up for air I say, "I never want you to feel alone again. I have your back if no one else does. I love you."

Chapter Twenty – Six
Macy

I stare at my reflection in the vanity mirror in our bathroom. The last night in this room because tomorrow, my big sister marries the man of her dreams. I could not think of a better man for her than Dylan.

My hand reaches up behind my neck. Taking off my necklace and then my earrings, a tear comes to the crease of my eye. It falls, sliding slowly down my cheek. I jump when a warm hand brushes it away.

"Mace." Jordan says, "Why are you crying?"

My hand goes to his wrist, while my eyes lock onto his, I sigh, "Tonight was a reminder of what could have been."

He takes a deep breath, "Macy, don't let your mind wander."

I turn, forcing space between us, and leave my back to him, "You broke my heart, Jordan. You promised me forever and took it away." I try to steady my breathing and control the tears that are wanting to profusely fall out of my eyes. My heart is breaking again and damn it, I tried so fucking hard to keep it from going back to this same heart break again.

"It's much more complicated than that." Jordan rubs his hand over my shoulder. "Don't let this ruin our last night in the same place together."

As much as I wanted to keep asking questions and let my mind take over, as much as I know I will regret this later, I let my heart have what it wants for the time being. I turn and let my lips crash to his and mold my body into his. I wrap my hands around his neck while his hands make a road map down my body. In one fluid motion, he scoops me up around my ass, and I wrap my legs around his body.

Jordan walks us to the bed while I am focused on trailing kisses down his neck and unbuttoning his shirt. Thankfully, he had already discarded his tie before entering the bathroom. I got a glimpse of it laying on the chair across from the bed. He slowly drops me to the bed. Kneeling, he takes off my heels one foot at a time, taking his time unbuttoning the straps.

Once he discards my shoes, he takes my arm and pulls me up to stand and twists me around, making me face the bed. "How much do you love this dress?" He asks.

I cock an eyebrow, "It was bought specifically for the rehearsal dinner."

The fabric starts ripping, tearing, and being pulled apart. Jordan lets it fall to the floor while he leans into my ear, "Remind me to buy you another one."

THE THINGS HIS WORDS DO TO ME.

I smirk, biting my lip.

He turns me to face him and crashes our lips back together; this time his tongue invades mine while he walks us back onto the bed. He unclasps my bra and tosses it across the room, making me giggle. Moving his lips from mine to my neck, shoulders, and down until he reaches my breasts, he takes one of my nipples into his mouth and sucks. I moan out in pleasurable pain.

"These have gotten bigger from what I recall." He smirks, tugging the other one into his mouth.

I moan, "Well, considering I was still a teenager back then, I'd say so."

He lets out a horse laugh and then, he sucks.

Moving his hands down to my panties, he dips them inside, running his fingers over me, making my eyes flutter. In no time, his hands are removed and moving up to my lips, "Suck." He orders, and I obey while watching his eyes twinkle with arousal.

"Someone has gotten dirtier in his older age." I grin.

"I'd say the same about you." He says while leaning up to kiss my lips softly.

"Mhm, I've missed your taste." His words make my pussy throb.

Then, without warning, He plunges his fingers back in my underwear and pushes one inside me, making my back buck and my moans become louder.

"Oh how I have missed you." Jordan says while watching me moan under his touch.

Another finger enters and my moans become so erotic, he places a hand over my mouth to keep from waking the entire house. Then he looks at me curiously, "Macy…. Have you not been having sex?" He pauses, "I almost asked the other night, but decided better of it."

I shake my head, "Not since you."

Like an animal, a primal growl comes out of him and within seconds, his pants are on the floor, and he is removing my underwear, "You don't even know how much I have missed you."

My eyes shoot up at him, confused and shocked. Tears swell in my eyes at the emotions I am feeling in my chest.

"Do you have a condom?" He asks.

I look at him dumbfounded, "Why would I have one? Plus, we did not use one the other night."

He chuckles, "Well I don't have one either."

I contemplate for a moment, but finally grab him with both hands, locking eyes with this man who stole my heart so many years ago. "I don't care. I just want you."

That is all the consent he needed as he works his fingers a little more in me, thrusting in and out to loosen me up and then he lines the head of his cock to my entrance. It's a lot bigger than I remember and my eyes widen, "You are bigger than I remember too."

His grin turns cocky, "Deep breaths baby, I'm going to stretch you."

He presses into me, a little inch at a time, allowing me to adjust to his size. A wave of emotion enters my core and as my eyes look into his. I see it in him too. I'm back where I belong.

Once he is all the way in, Jordan bends down, kissing me softly while he pulls out and pushes back in, all the way this time. "Mace" He starts, his body shaking, "I love you."

The emotions I feel in my core make a single tear slide down my cheek; his words, his thrusting and size, this week, it all has made me remember why I loved him to begin with, why he was my best friend, and why I wanted to grow old with him − protect him. "I love you too." I tell him as my release pours over me, making my toes curl and sucking his out of him. He releases in me and I feel every last bit of it.

Chapter Twenty-Seven
Macy

Jordan's heart beats into my ear while my head lays on his chest. His hand runs up and down my arm making my skin tingle. Closing my eyes, I take in my emotions and the fact I betrayed every ounce of self control I thought I had around him. When I arrived earlier this week and saw him, I never would have dreamed I would end up here right now, in his arms.

His lips kiss my forehead and for a moment, he lingers as if he's trying to soak it all in too.

I finally take a big breath and look up at him, "So where do we go from here?" I ask out of the blue.

That's when I see it. For just a moment, I see panic in his eyes before he closes them and turns his head away from me. Using my elbow to balance myself, I sit up, looking at him curiously. "What's wrong, Jordan?"

It's obvious now that he would rather look anywhere else but at me.

"Jordan. What is wrong?" I demand.

He sighs, turning his head to me, and when his eye lock onto mine, I notice he has a single tear in the corner of his eye. He kisses my forehead again, lingering longer than the one he just did.

"Macy," He starts, "After tomorrow, you need to go on with your life without me."

I'm stunned, looking at him, I replay the words over and over again, then ask, "Did I just hear you say what I think you did?"

Jordan removes himself out from under me and sits up on the side of the bed, running his hands through his hair nervously, before he stands and puts his boxers on.

"Explain yourself." I yell. "Explain why you just had sex with me, told me you loved me, and now you are telling me we cannot be together again." I pause, taking a big breath before whispering, "Jordan, you said you loved me."

"And I do." He starts but I interrupt him, "You do not love me, Jordan. You are a selfish bastard. I knew better than to let my guard down around you."

"Macy, I wish I could explain, but it's for your own good." He tries to exclaim.

"No. Don't you dare use that line. That's the same line you used on me when we were teenagers. That's the same line you broke my heart over. And here you are, doing it again. Fuck you, Jordan. FUCK YOU!!"

I grab my pajamas and put them on before running out of the room, down the hall to my sister's room.

Knocking on the door, it opens, and Dylan is standing there, looking shocked to see me.

"Mace?" He asks concerned.

I wipe a tear, "I-I'm sorry. If I'm interrupting, I can go. I just wanted to talk to Paige."

"Macy," My sister comes into view, "I don't care what was going on, you are always a priority to me. Come in, talk to me." She grabs my wrist and brings me inside her bedroom. I let out a breath of relief once the door closes behind me.

Dylan sits in the chair across from the bed as I explain to my sister what happened, Dylan stands, walking towards the door, "Dylan…" I pout, "Please don't kill him."

"I just want to go talk to him." He turns and kisses Paige, "You need to tell her." He says, pointing at me as she nods.

He gives me a comforting smile and grabs the door knob, leaving us in the room alone.

Once he is gone, I look at my sister confused, "Tell me what?"

She sighs, "For the record, what I'm about to tell you, I need you to know I did not know about this until literally just an hour ago. If I had known back then, I would have killed him myself."

I grab her hand, "Paige, what is going on?"

Her thumb rubs across mine, and finally after a moment, she looks up at me with a tear in her eye, "Do you remember the day Jordan broke up with you?"

I nod, of course I do…that was the day my whole world turned up side down.

We cannot be together anymore, Mace.

Go on and live your life without me.

You deserve someone better, someone other than me.

This is the only way.

Go live your life. I love you.

My heart starts hammering in my chest, "There is so much you do not know about that day, Mace. So much that I wish I would have known too." Paige says in an almost whisper.

"I swear to God, Paige. Spit it out." I order her.

"Jordan had no other choice, Macy. He was threatened with your life if he kept on dating you." She finally says.

My mouth falls open, "Who would do that? Who would hate him so much that they would want him to hurt me, the person he cared the most about?"

Her eyes told me the truth as they stared back into me, "That fucker!" I yell, but then pause, "But that does not excuse that he just did it to me again. I mean, his father has been in jail for years now. Why would he even do it again if my safety was no longer in question. He was just needing a good lay this weekend is all, and he got it." A tear wells in my eyes.

I lean into my sister, her arms embrace me in a hug while the tears flow down my cheeks.

***

Jordan

It is for the best, keeping her safe, no matter what my heart wants. No matter how much my heart is breaking watching her leave the room crying.

The door eases open and I spring to my feet hoping it's Macy, but I am disappointed to see Dylan walk through the door, "Oh, its just you."

"Well, that's no way to say hello to your best friend." He jokes.

I ignore him, sitting back down on the side of the bed with my head in my hands.

Dylan sighs, "Jordan, what did you think was going to happen when you started messing with her again?" He sits down at the chair across the bed, "Man, y'all were soul mates. I knew before you even told me that you loved her." He shakes his head, "It's not fair."

I look up at him, my eyes red with tears, "It fucking sucks."

Dylan is quiet for a moment, then says, "Paige is telling her the truth."

I look at him in a panic, "Which one?"

"The one where she finds out why you left all those years ago." He stares back at me. "She doesn't need to know this one."

I nod, agreeing, "The less she knows, the better."

"Yep." Dylan says in a clipped tone, "Are you sure about this? Are you sure it's worth giving her up a second time? You aren't a child anymore, Jordan. You have resources, people that will back you."

My leg shakes uncontrollably, "Yeah, but he's got more."

Chapter Twenty- Eight
Macy
16 years old

"I love you, silly boy." I tell Jordan, kissing his nose. We are laying in my bedroom on the bed cuddling. He stayed with me again this weekend; his father is home and my parents are out of town. It's become our thing when they are gone, he normally stays the whole weekend with me.

"I love you too." Jordan smiles.

We have baked cookies, watched our favorite tv shows, and made love. Over and over all weekend. He even ran me a bath last night and sat in the tub with me. Nothing physical, just mentally intimate. I'm falling more in love with him everyday.

I still think about the night on the ridge, how he thought he was better off not here anymore and how one small decision I made to go up there stopped him from doing it. Sometimes, people just want to feel like they have someone.

"Macy?" Jordan questions me.

"Hmmm?" I look at him.

"What do you think about when you think of our future?" He whispers.

My eyes stare at him in shock, "A house full of little versions of us."

"Yes." He agrees, "We could have our own home like your parents, a few kids, and I fully intend to be nothing like my father to them. I want to be like your dad is to you and Paige." He says nonchalantly.

"You will be the best husband and father some day." I assure him.

"To you and our kids. I promise you Mace, I'm going to marry you." He grins at me.

I nuzzle into him even more as we lay in bed and cuddle.

He is my home and my safe place.

"I wonder if we could get your dad a discount if we got married the same day as Dylan and Paige?" Jordan chuckles, "I'm sure he would appreciate the thought."

I laugh, "I'm sure he would be all for it."

"Have you decided on a college yet?" I ask him.

"I think I have decided to take the offer from Colorado State and get my engineering degree. Your dad is always telling me it's a great field to go into and I would be good at it." He pauses, rubbing my arm, "Plus, it would be a good income for us to start our lives with."

I smile at the thought, "Do you always make decisions with me in mind?" I ask him.

"Sure do. It's you and me, Mace." He kisses my forehead.

I snuggle more into him with my head over his heart, listening to the sound of it beat.

Chapter Twenty- Nine
Macy
Present

I fell asleep in Paige's room last night. We laid in bed and talked about a lot of things, reminiscing on childhood memories. One last sleepover, just her and I, was what my heart needed.

Even though I always thought our wedding day's would be close together and to two *brothers;* I am still happy for her and Dylan and their happily ever after.

I just hope mine is somewhere in the future.

Jordan

Ding

It's the morning of the wedding, I wake to an empty bed and a bruised heart.

Ding.

My phone dings again to alert me of a text message; I groan and grab it.

We cannot pin point his location. He made bail earlier this week. Inmates are saying he talked about finding her and finishing what he started.

My heart hammers in my chest; he could be here. He could be anywhere.

I jump up out of bed and rush to Dylan's room. My fist hits it with powerful force, and I don't stop until it flies open.

An irritated Dylan stands at the opening, in nothing but boxer shorts, and a *I'm about to whoop your ass* facial expression.

I push past him, ignoring his groan.

"They cannot pin point his exact location." My tone rings through the room in a panic.

Dylan, now wide eyed and awake from the news, "What the hell kind of private investigator did you pay if he cannot do his job when lives are on the line." He quips.

"One that will not be getting his full pay out if he does not get his shit together." I exclaim.

Dylan nods in agreement, "So what's the plan brother?" he asks.

"We need to go tell Brian." I state.

Dylan puts clothes on and follows me to Brian and Kristina's room. Hesitant for a moment, I slowly knock. "Give me a minute." A sleepy Brian calls from the other side of the door.

After a moment, it slowly opens and Brian stands, eyeing us in a robe. I can hear their shower running which means we either interrupted something that I do not want to think about, or we woke him up.

I'm going to go with the latter.

"This better be good. I was just about to get in the shower with my wife." Brian grumbles.

I swallow down the vomit in my throat. Don't get me wrong, Kristina is a beautiful woman, but these people are like parents to me; it's disgusting thinking of them this way.

"Sorry, Brian," Dylan starts, "but this could not wait."

He gestures for us to come in and closes the bathroom door, telling his wife to stay in there when she got out, announcing our arrival.

"Well, spit it out." He orders.

"Umm, I have probable cause that Macy may be in danger, sir." I finally say.

His eyes dart to me, "And why do you think this?" He asks.

"Because when my father was booked into the jail he has resided in for the past several years, I hired a special detective to keep tabs on him from the inside. What he said and what his plans were when he got out. I wanted to know immediately when he was going to be up for parole." I tell Brian.

He eyes me to go on.

"Well sir, the whole reason I'm even here for the wedding this weekend, is because I got a message explaining that my father was up for parole and would be out on the streets the same week of the wedding." I eye Dylan who gestures for me to go on, "And I was told that he plans to finish what he started as soon as he gets out."

Brian's face falls, full of fear, "You are telling me my daughter is no longer safe?" His tone is full of anger.

I shake my head no.

"And of all days, on my other daughter's wedding day." He shakes his head and grabs his phone.

"Who are you calling?" Dylan asks.

"Letting security for venue know we need them on alert for the day. I want you two with Paige and Macy at all times, do you understand me? I do not care if they go to the bathroom, you go with them." Brian orders us.

My eyes go to Dylan, and Brian asks, "What's wrong now?"

I cough, telling Dylan to take control on this one.

"Well, you see, Jordan here broke Macy's heart again last night. He told her he couldn't be with her after today." Dylan tells Brian.

"Jordan." Brian says in a clipped tone.

"Yes sir." I answer, almost in a whisper.

"Remind me to kick your ass later." He looks at me sternly, "But right now, just keep her safe."

I nod in agreement, "I'll die before someone hurts her sir."

"What about if you hurt her? Will you die then? Or do you get a pass?" He verbally jabs at me.

Ouch.

I deserved that.

Brian takes a deep breath, "Boy, I raised you better than this. Make it up to her, or so help me, once we deal with your father, I'll deal with you." Kristina's voice calls for her husband on the other side of the door, "Keep this between us three." Brian orders, "No need to instill panic. We will get through today with ease. I'll beef up security and us three will protect the women we love." He calls after his wife to wait a minute and then says, "Now, go."

Dylan and I nod, walking out of the room as the door slams shut behind us, making us both jump.

"What now?" Dylan asks.

"You are getting married today brother. Go focus on that. I'll watch after the girls until time to be at the church. You can't see Paige anyways. It's bad luck." I say.

"Right." He takes a deep breath, "Surely that fucker wont show up today."

The memory of my father fades in. The bastard got what he deserved the day he was locked up. It was originally for drugs after Christmas Day, but Macy's father finally talked her into pressing charges for the creamery where he attacked her and Paige. He was able to pull video footage of the incident and get him locked up for abuse on a minor and premeditation of rape on a minor since he was pulling at her clothing. However, his good behavior from being in jail landed him a parole plea. I never went to visit him and I damn sure never intended to see him again, but I knew he was dangerous. Macy had threatened him, and he knew the only way to keep her quiet was to end her life. If he harmed her, he knew it would harm me. Basically, killing two birds with one stone. I hired a private detective soon after high school with my mother's life insurance money until I was able to afford one myself. My father was not one to forgive a threat easily and when Macy threatened him that day on our front porch, he had someone new on his radar of brutal beatings.

174

Over my dead body will I let him get close to her, I do not care how pissed off she is at me.

***

Macy

For some reason, Jordan decided he was going to ride with all of us bridesmaids in Mary's suburban while the rest of the groomsmen rode with my parents and Dylan in their SUV. My dad was very pushy on letting Jordan ride with us so, ultimately, there was no way around it. My father does not push his stern tone and looks much but when he does, he means business and you do not push back.

I sit in the front seat where there's less availability for Jordan to try to sit beside me. Glancing in the back seat, I notice how uncomfortable he seems sitting in between Rylee and Elizabeth. His eyes meet mine, and a soft smile comes over him when his eyes lock onto mine. I quickly turn back to the front. I refuse to let him get a one up on me again. I thought he had changed, I thought he was a good man now after the time we had spent together this week. After last night, I've come to the conclusion that he is the not so best man after all.

"Here we are ladies." Mary says, pulling up to the side of the venue. "Go in through those doors," she points to some side doors and we all nod, looking at them and telling her thank you. "Your dresses and shoes are all in there as well. I'm going to park and will meet y'all inside." She says, and eyes Jordan, "Make sure they all get inside and then you will take the stairs. Go up one floor and the groomsmen's room is on the right as soon as you reach the floor."

I notice he nods and waits until we are all out before closing the door and gesturing us to go on inside. I make a quick note of the Christmas Decorations outside. Candy Canes and Flowers line the sidewalk around the side of the Venue in the most beautiful walking path.

Following my sister inside, the bridesmaids follow behind us and into a beautiful room with mirrors surrounding one side of the room, a couch, and a restroom. Our emerald green floor length dresses are all hanging up on the wall with our shoes under them. Paige's beautiful wedding gown and veil hangs in the middle of them.

"This place is beautiful." Paige says.

"Is this the bride's room?" A lady says while popping her head inside.

"Yes?" I answer.

Another woman steps in behind her and they both carry big cameras and bags on their backs; obviously, the wedding photographer.

"We are the photographers. Mind if we start in here with you all?" The first lady asks.

"Sure!" Paige beams.

They fully walk in the room, getting to know each of our names and talking to Paige some.

"You are going to love your wedding photo album" one of the lady's smirks at Paige weirdly.

"Oh, I cannot wait to see them and get some printed for the house." Paige says giddily.

"You are most definitely going to want copies of a bunch of them." she smirks again.

I look around, suddenly realizing I forgot my makeup bag in Mary's car.

"I'll be back." I tell my sister. "Maybe I can stop Mary before she locks her car, my makeup bag is in there."

Making my way out the doors we came in, and across the road to the parking lot, someone stops me. They seem familiar, but I cannot seem to place where I know them.

"You're Macy, correct?" The woman asks.

"Umm, yes?" I question confused.

"You probably do not remember me." The woman laughs, "I'm Kyla, the elf you all met at the escape room."

"Oh." I say shocked. She looks totally different now. No scary elf makeup or clothing. Her hair is down straight, and makeup covers her face. She's also wearing a floral dress and heels.

"Are you coming to the wedding?" I ask

She nods, yes, and says, "My apologies. My aunt is Mary. She needed extra hands today making sure everything was going smooth and I have the day off."

Ah. That makes sense.

"Well, I hope you enjoy it. She did an amazing job setting everything up." I tell Kyla. Then I ask, "Is...Pinky with you?" I ask stumbling over the other elf's name.

"Yeah, she is my sister." She smiles, "She is around here somewhere."

This family makes so much sense now. I remind myself to keep my facial expression neutral.

"Well, good to meet you outside of your elf costume." I smile, "I am in a hurry, so I better get on to where I was going so I can get back."

"Okay!" Kyla grins, "By the way, the video of you and your guy is hilarious when it gets to the part of your friends walking in." She laughs and walks off, leaving me horrified.

I need to hire someone to permanently erase it forever.

"Shit." I say, turning quickly to try to catch Kyla so I can ask her to get her aunt to open her car for me but as soon as I turn around, I collide with a thick chest and a hand goes around my forearm.

"Miss me?" The deep voice says.

Chapter Thirty
Jordan

After we all exited Mary's SUV, I made sure all the women got into their room and settled before leaving them to take the stairs up to the groomsmen's room. Stopping a security guard on my way up the stairs, I told him to make sure no women went in or out of that room unless I gave them the okay.

"How do I look?" Dylan asks me, turning from his mirror, wearing a full tux, shoes, and tie.

I laugh, "The ugliest human being I've ever met. God help your wife."

Dylan grabs the box of Kleenex laying on the table beside him and throws them right at my head.

"Come on, Dylan. You lost your athletic touch already? Man you are getting old." I joke.

"How about you stop talking crap and go check on our women." Dylan states, laughing.

I nod, agreeing. Turning to the mirror behind me, I fix my tie and grin, this is going to be a good day.

Hurrying down the stairs, I hear a commotion from the hallway in front of the bridesmaid's room.

It's Paige.

"That is bullshit. I need to find my sister." She yells at the security guard, who now has a hand on Paige's forearm.

"Let her go." I yell at him.

"But sir, you said no one could leave the room." He looks at me confused.

"Apparently one did. Where is Macy?" I ask him.

The man lets go of Paige's arm and she runs over to me, grabbing my tux, "Jordan, she left a while ago. She was going out to get her makeup bag from Mary's SUV and she never came back." Paige is on the verge of a panic attack.

I pull her over to the side and whisper, "Listen to me carefully. All of you ladies stay in this room. Door shut and locked. Do not let anyone else in this room unless it is me or your father. Do you understand?"

She looks at me worried, "What is going on, Jordan?"

I take a deep breath, "Paige, just do as I say."

She nods, "Okay."

I turn to the security guard soon as Paige goes in the room and shuts the door, "So help me, you better not let a single soul in that room unless I okay it. Tackle anyone who tries to get in without my knowledge. Do you understand me?" I ask him.

He nods, standing in front of the door.

I turn, heading towards the doors the girls arrived inside the venue through; my feet falter seeing a man standing in front of me holding on to my girl's forearm so tight her arm's almost blue from no blood being able to flow.

"Allen." I say in a clipped tone, "What the actual fuck are you doing here?"

My father smirks, "No proper greeting for your old man? Pity, I'll just have to get one out of your girl here." He runs a finger down her cheek, "Oh wait, she's not your girl anymore. Is she?"

Macy snarls at him. Something in my chest tightens; proud of her for being stubborn and standing her ground, but I also know the type of man my father is and she's only testing the bull.

A memory over takes me:

Jordan
17 years old
Christmas Eve

My mother is working late tonight to try catching up on bills. My father has been in and out a few times. Thankfully, I have been safe at Macy or Dylan's every time he has came home.

Putting away my dinner, I load the dishwasher and turn it on to run sometime during the night.

Bang

The front door slams open, making me jump and turn to see what made it hit the wall of the living room.

My heart rate accelerates when I see my father standing by the door frame, beer in hand, and looking at me like he hates me.

"Your little bitch has a mouth on her." He says sternly. "Threatening me with calling the cops if I do not leave her alone."

I try to ignore him while I continue cleaning up the kitchen.

"Look at me when I am speaking to you boy." He slams his fist on the kitchen counter.

I look up, "I have no control over what she says." I finally admit.

Allen ponders for a moment, and then says, "You better let her know she has no idea who she is messing with. If she comes at me again, I will kill her. Do you understand me?"

My eyes shoot up at him, "You touch her and I'll make sure you rot in a jail cell."

He laughs, "Ah, young love. Not worth your time, boy. Every pussy is the same as the last." He stares at me, "I mean it. As long as you two are together, she's on the chopping block."

My eyes search his, "What does being together have to do with anything?"

He grins, an evil grin, "Why would I want you to be happy when you did nothing but ruin my life? I never wanted you. You can live a miserable life for all I care. If she is a part of your life, then she's on that chopping block with you."

It feels like my heart just ripped apart into a million pieces. For the first time since I came into this world, my father chose not to hit me. Instead, he did something so much worse.

He just made a decision for me that will forever break my heart.

Chapter Thirty – One
Macy
Christmas Day
16 years old

It's been a few weeks since I threatened Jordan's father on their front porch, and I meant every word. I can still see the scared boy standing on that ridge, ready to end it all because he thought no one cared about him. His own mother did not stand up for him. By God, if no one else will do it, I plan to.

I woke up Christmas morning full of hope for today and so excited to spend Christmas with Jordan here at my house. He is supposed to be coming over this morning and celebrating with my family and I.

Jumping up out of bed, I grab my comfy clothes I laid out the night before to lounge in today, head to my bathroom to wash my face and brush my teeth, pull my hair back in a loose ponytail, and head downstairs to the kitchen. My mother is already cooking up a storm for our Christmas breakfast, dad is sitting at the bar drinking coffee, our Christmas tree is lit up and gifts all around it and the Christmas story is playing on the tv in the living room – our yearly tradition.

"Where's Paige?" I ask looking around. My sister is normally up before everyone on Christmas. It is her favorite holiday. She swears she will get married on Christmas Day some day.

"She went to Dylan's this morning to give him his gifts since he won't be able to come by today. They have a Christmas at his aunt's house." Mom replies as she scrambles eggs.

I nod, and say, "Jordan should be here anytime. I told him to come on over in time to eat."

My dad sits his coffee cup down, "You make sure he knows he is always welcome here anytime, Mace. I know his mom works a lot and his piece of shit father is never around."

I laugh, "Yes sir, thank you daddy.

A knock is heard at the door, and I walk over with a giant smile, it slowly fades when I see Jordan's face. It looks like he has been crying.

"Jordan?" I question him, "What's wrong? Come inside."

He shakes his head no, and finally says, "Macy, I need to talk to you. Can you come out here? I'm not planning on staying long."

I feel my adrenaline spike through my veins, but reply, "Uhm, sure?"

Grabbing my coat and slipping on my house shoes that I leave by the front door, I tell my parents I'll be right back and walk out the front door with Jordan, pulling the door closed behind me.

Once the door is shut, he takes my hands in his and leans in, kissing me deeply. He is hesitant when we break away from each other.

"Jordan? What is wrong?" I ask concerned.

"Macy, I need you to go on and live your life. Go to college, make friends, date other people. I need you to live without me." His shaky voice tells me.

I blink rapidly, trying to process the words he is saying.

"Excuse me?" I ask him, "You are kidding right now? It is fucking Christmas, Jordan."

He kisses my forehead, "I mean it Mace. I love you but we cannot be together. Please go live your life."

A tear flows down my cheek, "Jordan. My life is you."

He looks at the ground but his voice breaks, "Not anymore."

And before I know it, he sits a box at my feet and turns to walk away. I stand in shock and watch him drive off. Realizing he left something at my feet, I bend down and open it. It's a smaller box, and inside there is a note that says, "Macy, I will always love you. I wish things could be different. Just remember, you saved me. I hope you know I will return the favor. I love you."

Macy
Present

This man really annoys me. I did not leave this place to go off to college just to come back home and his ass come back for me. I thought he was dead because I have not heard of or seen him in years. I know my father had him put in jail after he hit me, but that's the last time he has been mentioned or seen. It is comical really. He is just throwing a damn temper tantrum because I threatened him as a teenager. You know what they say about men with little dicks; they throw the biggest tantrums because of little man syndrome.

His wife was afraid of him, but I was not. Nor am I now. His hold on my forearm is really starting to piss me off too. What man on God's green earth thinks he is allowed to hold on to a woman like this?

186

Jordan is looking at us, fist clenched, and his jawline rigid.

His Tux looks so good on him; it honestly turns me on seeing him like this.

Damn Mace, shut the hell up- I tell my brain *—you are in a death grip of a man who is dangerous and this is what you think of?*

I chuckle and Allen looks at me, "What are you laughing at girl?"

My eyes widen, that laugh was supposed to stay inside my brain.

I am officially losing it.

I feel him force me backwards towards our exit, and Jordan takes a step forward.

"Don't move boy. You would not want anything to happen to your first love, would you?" He snarls at Jordan, pulling me closer to the door.

"Macy, stay calm." Jordan tells me.

"Thanks captain obvious. That was my first intention." I answer sarcastically, rolling my eyes.

With our back towards the door, Allen kicks it open with his foot and pulls us out through it.

BANG

Allen's grip on my arm instantly releases and I fall to the ground. Jordan runs out the door and right to me, grabbing my hands and helping me up.

"What the fuck!" Allen growls.

"I think we figured out who kidnapped Santa guys." Kyla says to a group of elves standing behind her. "Thanks for the backup Elves!" She says to her friends while holding a big candy cane that she knocked Allen in the head with as we came out the door, making him lose his hold on me.

Pinky, Kyla's sister – I really need to learn her real name – walks over to me, "I am so glad you are okay!!"

Paige and the bridesmaids, the venue's security guards, along with my father, mother, Dylan, and the groomsmen, all come running out the exit too. Paige grabs me in a big bear hug, "Oh Macy, I am so glad you are okay!!"

Everyone huddles around me, each taking their time hugging me while Kyla holds her candy cane on Allen, begging him to try to run.

"You all are creepy as hell." Allen snarls, "What kind of wedding is this?"

My father walks over to him, "One that you were not invited to." He leans back and punches Allen in the head.

Sirens are heard off in the distance. I look through the crowd of people, wondering who called the police, and my sister smiles, "I called 911 when Jordan put us back in the room. I called Dad and Dylan too. I was going to make sure you were going to have back up."

I give her a big bear hug. Finally tearing away from my sister's embrace when I hear Jordan's voice.

"This is for making me break up with Macy all those years ago and this is for trying to hurt her now." Jordan says to his father, giving his father two punches to the face.

I ease my way over to Jordan, "What do you mean making you break up with me?"

He looks at me with embarrassment, "He threatened your life all those years ago, Mace. I was a kid back then, I could not risk it. Your life was just beginning and I was the one in the way of it. My love for you was so deep, I did not want to be the one to stop you from living when you were the reason I was living to begin with." He pauses, "I knew if he got out of jail, he would be trying to find you. I had to make sure I was here at the wedding to protect you but I knew if he found out we were seeing one another again, he would try to end us both. I am so sorry, Mace.

Tears prick my eyes. Here I was thinking he was the not so best man, when in reality, he was the best man I could have ever given my heart to. He was protecting me in ways I did not even know of.

Chapter Thirty- Two
Jordan

The detective that I had hired, police officers, and other first responders all surrounded the venue within just a couple of minutes after Kyla knocked the shit out of Allen with the candy cane. Honestly, it sounds cliché, but the fact that she plays an elf for a job and knocked a guy out with a candy cane was hilarious after it was all said and done.

The venue has cameras up that the dumbass did not think about cutting off, so the police force was able to see exactly when he arrived, when he took Macy, and how the whole incident went down. At first, they did not like that Brian and I both took swings at Allen, but they eventually said, *off the record,* they would do the same for the ones they loved.

Brian and I did not care. Hand cuff us for all we care. The bastard deserved it. And I'd do it all again where Macy was concerned.

I explained to Macy the reality of what happened the night my father told me she was on the chopping block too. It felt like a weight had been lifted off my chest when she hugged me. If I had the resources I have now back then, I would have never even done it. I would have never ruined her Christmas morning and made her hate Christmas all these years because of it. Looking back on it, I was just a kid myself who should have never been put in that situation.

"We have what we need to keep him locked up for good." The detective tells me, shaking my hand and checking on Macy, "Are you sure you are okay Miss?" He asks her.

She nods, "Yes, thank you again."

He smiles and Brian walks up to shake his hand too, "Thank you for alerting Jordan about Allen's tendencies."

"I'm just grateful Mr. Smith has given me a job all these years." He says and I cough, letting him know to keep quiet, but Macy looks up at me, "All these years?" She questions him.

"Yes, ma'am. Mr. Smith has hired me to keep an eye on you and Allen's whereabouts since he graduated college." He smiles, "Your safety has always been my top priority."

He grins at me, and I glare at him, "We will talk later."

He laughs and leans into Macy, "The man is crazy in love with you."

Her eyes twinkle up at me and I clear my throat.

Brian says, "Well, now I feel like the third wheel. I'll see you guys inside."

Macy hugs her father, "Thank you daddy."

"Anything for my girl." Brian says rubbing her back. Once they pull out of their hug, he puts his hand out for me, "Jordan, I hope you know you have my respect son."

A tear forms at the corner of my left eye, "Thank you, sir."

Brian leaves Macy and I on the sidewalk. Everyone else has slowly made their way back inside to get ready for a wedding that Paige says we are already running behind for.

Macy's hand goes to my tux jacket, and she pulls me into her, "Mr. Smith. Would you be so kind as to walk me down the aisle this evening?" She asks me with a smile.

I laugh, "Thought I didn't have a choice?"

She rolls her eyes and I smile, "You know my answer will always be yes."

Raising up on her tip toes, Macy's lips crash onto mine, and for a minute, I feel like we are floating in our own bubble.

***

Macy

The wedding was beautiful. Guests all started arriving shortly after the police cars drove off with Jordan's father. I am grateful that I will never have to worry about him again. He deserves to spend the rest of his days behind bars.

"Macy!" Kyla hollers at me from a few tables over, and I walk over to her, "How are you doing?" She asks.

I smile, "Much better, and thank you by the way. How did you know we were there?" I ask.

She leans into me and whispers, "I saw him walking around the side of the building before I spoke to you in the parking lot. I thought he looked out of place. Then when I made my way inside, I overheard your sister panicking and calling your father." She pauses, taking a breath, "I knew some of my friends who work at the escape room with me were near by and going into work tonight, so I asked them to come as back up. They are my ride or dies." Picking up her water, she takes a sip, "We snuck around the side of the building and waited near the bushes. I could see his death grip on you outside the door and Jordan looked pissed. I knew he was trying to get away and made a decision to hit him in the head with the closest thing I could find. Ironically enough, it was one of your sister's candy canes she had as decoration outside the venue." She chuckles, "I guess I was in the right place at the right time."

I shake my head yes, "Absolutely you were! I am so thankful for your listening ears." My cheeks blush, "I am sorry again about the PDA video in the escape room."

Her eyebrow raises, "Honey, that was not just PDA. That man knew what he was doing."

I blush, "Please tell me y'all are a thing." She gestures to Jordan, who is now making his way to me.

"That is up to her." Jordan smiles, his arm going around my waist.

"Excuse us." I tell Kyla.

"Y'all should totally make an Only fans. You could make a killing off it!" She winks and I blush again.

Jordan looks at me curiously, "What the heck did she mean by that?"

"Ummm, they all watched the cameras of us getting it on." I tell him.

"You mean me getting you off?" He jokes.

I hit his shoulder with a slap and he laughs.

"Sooo," he starts, "What was you going to reply when she asked if we were a thing?"

I smile, "Before you so effectively interrupted a private conversation…" I roll my eyes, "I was going to tell her that I was hoping we get our second chance."

Jordan's eyes twinkle at me, full of hope and dreams. He leans into me and says, "I'm going to show you how good of a man I can be for you, Mace. Starting with this…"

The not so Best Man

His lips crash onto mine; maybe I can start loving Christmas again after all.

Epilogue
1 year later
Macy

"If you do not get your ass down here in five minutes, I am going to go crazy pregnant lady on you!" Paige's voice rings down from the bottom of the stairs of my parents' house. I fully moved everything home from College this year and moved back in with my parents. Even though Jordan has his own place, I did not want to fully move in together until we got engaged or even married. I spent so much time during college away from home and my parents, I wanted to make up my time of missing them.

"I'm coming." I yell down the stairs from my room. Paige, Dylan, Jordan and I are all going out on a double date this evening for Paige and Dylan's anniversary. It's Christmas Day and the boys have a surprise date for us.

Paige is smiling extra big as I get to the bottom of the steps, "What is your deal?" I ask, irritated. "Your pregnancy hormones making you like this today?" I ask.

She laughs, "Yep. Totally the pregnancy hormones."

We grab our purses and turn the lights off before walking out the front door.

"Mom and dad said to tell you not to wait up for them tonight. They may stay in Aspen." Paige says, sliding into my car.

I make a puke face knowing exactly what that means. They have a child living at home again so they have to go off if they want to have sex.

"Where am I driving to?" I ask my sister.

Paige picks up her phone and scrolls through her texts, "I do not recognize this address." She says, showing me the destination.

I cock my head to the side, and then it clicks with me where that will take us, "The ridge?" I ask.

"I guess." She shrugs.

Thankfully, it has not been snowing this week or I do not think my car would make it up there, and I know Paige would not be able to walk the whole way.

I put some music on and Paige and I chat about my little niece or nephew and nursery plans as I follow the GPS.

I'm careful driving up to the top, grateful that the state has come in and made the road accessible now and a lot safer, but it still makes me anxious. They even made a parking lot at the top.

"There is more cars up here than normal." I comment, getting out of my car after parking it, but Paige ignores me walking on up ahead.

"Slow down!" I yell at her, but my feet freeze.

I drop my keys, too stunned for muscle movement at the sight before me.

"Come on, Mace. Your forever awaits." Paige squeals.

My parents, Dylan, and Paige all stand beside the ridge where I met Jordan all those years ago. He stands in front of the rock he stood on that night in blue jeans and a green button up. Roses lined all around him in a circle and candles are spread out along the ridge.

My father walks up to me and hugs me, snapping me out of my shock.

"Daddy," I say hoarsely, "Is this what I think it is?"

He nods, "He is the best man for you, Mace. I would be honored for him to become my son in law. He is already my son at heart."

Tears stream down my face, and my body starts to shake with adrenaline. My father steps beside me, wrapping his hand in mine, and leads me to the man of my dreams.

The last year has been amazing with him. We have reconnected in all the ways my heart needed. We have talked about the past, the present, and the future. I knew this day was coming, but I was not expecting it today.

My father stops us in front of Jordan, and he smiles letting go of my hand and steps back beside my mother. Jordan takes my hand and leads us into the circle of roses together.

His thumb runs over my mine and our eyes lock, "Macy," he starts, "when I met you for the first time on this ridge, I was a scared boy. I did not feel loved or wanted. I truly did not want to live life anymore." He takes a deep breath, "But for some reason, on that specific night, you showed up out of the blue and stopped me from doing something stupid. You saved my life that night." A tear scrolls down his face, "That night, you gave me a reason to keep living. When I saw you again in high school, I knew that some higher power was pulling us together." He takes a few deep breaths, "Then I lost you and I truly did not know how I was going to go on. But somehow, we made our way together again. When something is meant to be, you cannot stop it."

I smile, "I'm just too stubborn."

He laughs, "Amen."

Everyone around us giggles.

"You are my best friend, my heart, and my world. My life became sweeter the day you walked into it. You saved my life, Mace; in more than just physical. You are the air that I breathe, and you make me want to be the best man for you." He reaches into his back pocket and pulls out a black box. Opening it, he kneels down on one knee and asks, "Will you spend forever with me and become Mrs. Jordan Smith?"

My eyes widen at the ring that is shining before me but then they lock on the eyes of the man I love, the man who I gave my whole heart to so many years ago and who has owned it since. I nod, tears streaming down my face, "YES!"

He jumps up, taking the ring out of the box and placing it on my finger. Leaning into my ear he whispers, 'I hope this makes up for ruining your love for Christmas Day."

Acknowledgments

To my husband, for your unwavering support in all I do, thank you is an understatement. When the world seems heavy, you are there for me to lean on.

To my Editor, Pat, thank you for taking my writing and making it into something publishable. So thankful our paths crossed.

To my ARC readers, thank you for supporting me. Some of you have been with me since my first book and your continued support does not go unnoticed. I hope I can hug you all someday.

To my readers, whether you have bought the physical book or read it on your e-readers, thank you. Every book bought and page read, is building a dream for someone who just loves to write love stories. I have notebooks full of future books to come and I hope you enjoy them all.

About the Author

Please go to www.authorjdwhaley.com for more info about Jessica and links to her socials and newsletters list!